the misadventures of
NOBBIN SWILL

CL CKED!

LISA HARKRADER

YELLOW
JACKET

YELLOW JACKET
an imprint of Little Bee Books

New York, NY
Copyright © 2021 by Lisa Harkrader
All rights reserved, including the right of reproduction
in whole or in part in any form.
Yellow Jacket and associated colophon are trademarks of
Little Bee Books.
Manufactured in China RRD 0521
First Edition
10 9 8 7 6 5 4 3 2 1
Library of Congress Cataloging-in-Publication Data is available
upon request.

ISBN 978-1-4998-0975-6 (hardcover)
ISBN 978-1-4998-0976-3 (ebook)
yellowjacketreads.com

For information about special discounts on bulk purchases,
please contact Little Bee Books at sales@littlebeebooks.com.

For Heather and Lee, my childhood partners in crime

Contents

1

A Bag of Sand

Once upon a time, I was propped against a tilt rail, trying not to nod off during my official duties.

"Are you all right, your highness?" a voice called out.

My head jerked up. I blinked and rubbed sleep crust from my eyes.

Prince Charming had rousted us from our beds before the sun had cast its first pink glance over the kingdom. Now we were huddled on the training course behind the stables, hidden from the prying eyes of the castle. Shadows stretched before us. Wisps of early-morning mist snaked about the dew-slick grass at our feet. Beside me, Ulff yawned so wide, he looked to be swallowing his own head backward.

It was meant to be the five of us this morn:

1. The prince, of course
2. His faithful guard, Ulff
3. Sir Hugo, his trainer for all things princely
4. Darnell, his steadfast steed
5. And his loyal assistant, Nobbin (me)

But Princess Angelica had heard us creeping past her bedchamber in the wee hours and crept after us.

"To offer helpful hints," she'd told Charming.

And so we were six.

It was Sir Hugo's voice that had wrenched me from my slumber.

"Your highness?" he called again.

Charming trotted Darnell to the far end of the training tiltyard—the long, narrow patch behind the stables marked off for jousting practice. He raised the visor of his newly plumed helmet.

"I'm"—he wheezed out a cough—"in fine fettle, good sir. Fettle as a kettle." His voice, thin and raspy, drifted back to us on the crisp air. "Let us press on."

He clanked shut his visor.

I shot a look at Ulff. Ulff raised his eyebrows and shot a look back.

This would be Charming's sixth charge down the

list. He'd dropped his shield once, lost his lance twice, and missed the target entirely each and every time.

But he would not give up.

For this was no everyday prince training. It wasn't Charming simply brushing up on his gallantry or valor.

At stake this time was honor.

His *family's* honor.

The prince was training for the upcoming tournament. It was to be the spectacular closing event of the king's jubilee, a days-long celebration filled with balls and banquets, festivals and parades. The prince's family had won the jubilee tournaments for longer than anyone could remember—through his father, his father's father, his father before him, and many fathers before that. Now, it was Charming's turn.

He urged Darnell forward to the start of the list—the jousting course that ran the length of the tiltyard. Along both sides, Ulff and I had piled heaps of straw. To cushion the fall if—in truth, *when*—Charming tumbled from the saddle.

In the center, mounted to the tilt rail—the long fence that divided the two sides of the list—was the quintain. It was a jousting dummy on a swinging arm used as a stand-in for the opposing jouster.

Sir Hugo had put great care into the crafting of this quintain, thinking to better ready the prince for a true opponent. On the one side, the side Charming was to hit with his lance, Sir Hugo had fixed a wooden cutout of a knight holding a metal shield. The other side was weighted with a heavy sandbag hanging from a rope. When the jouster hit the shield with his lance, the sandbag swung around. If all went as planned, jouster and mount would by then be far past the quintain, and the bag would miss them entirely.

Charming reached into his armored gauntlet to pinch the mitten he'd tucked there for luck. He pushed the mitten back in, squared his shoulders, lifted his chin—

—then reached in again for another lucky pinch.

Sir Hugo shook his head.

"He has the skills," he said. "What he lacks is the confidence."

Angelica leaned over the tilt rail. "I could do it," she called to her brother, helpfully.

"She could at that," I said.

Ulff considered this. He raised his voice. "It would take the pressure off you," he told Charming.

"No." The prince raised his lance to its vertical starting position. "I'm the eldest. It is *my* duty. My responsibility. There's history to consider. Tradition. Not to mention our family's reputation. And, I daresay, my own. And of course, the tournament trophy and its rightful place at the heart of our castle. I can't let any of it slip away. Because it's . . . it's all of it"—he cleared his throat—"my responsibility."

He sat motionless in the saddle for a long moment, head lowered.

Then he blew out a breath and squared his shoulders once more. Sir Hugo dropped his flag, and Charming— lance gripped in one hand—gave a click with his tongue.

Darnell snorted, tossed his head, and set off, trotting at first, then gathering speed, until he was in full thunder: head down, hooves digging into the earth, every muscle in his body churning. Charming leaned into the gallop and lowered his lance, his plume whipping out behind him as he pounded closer, and closer still, looking every inch the valiant jouster—

—until, at the very last sliver of a moment, he flinched. Not a lot. Not so much most folks would notice.

But enough.

The tip of his lance glanced off the quintain's shield, the wooden knight swung back, and the sandbag spun around, thumping Charming square between the shoulders.

"Oooff!"

The prince pitched plume-first over Darnell's noble head. His lance stuck fast in the dirt, and Charming swung over it like a catapult in shining armor. For a moment, he seemed to hang there, suspended upside down over the grip of his lance, before finally toppling over.

He landed with a *clank!* in a pile of straw.

2

A Charm in the Library

Blight and bumblecrust!"

Charming wrenched the mitten from his gauntlet and chucked it in the straw.

And then, because he was Charming, he picked it up again, plucked out a strand of straw, and smoothed the mitten's threads.

He led Darnell to the stables for a brisk brush down and bucket of water. He left Angelica feeding and nuzzling the horses—both Darnell and her own sweet mare, Rounders—and strode off to the castle. His now-squashed plume bobbed limply above his helmet.

Ulff and I followed.

I stole a look at Ulff. He nodded, and I rustled a

scrap of parchment from my tunic. It was a list Ulff and I had made the night before, fearing Charming might need a bit of bucking up.

I started at the top of the list, at item #1.

Things to
Cheer Charming

1. You didn't look that bad.
2. Your form was excellent.
3. Once you get the form, your lance technique will ~~quickly~~ follow at some point.
4. Practice makes ~~perfect!~~ better!
5. If they awarded tournament cups for effort, you'd win for sure.

"It wasn't that bad," I told the prince, or rather, the prince's backside.

I held the parchment toward Ulff and pointed to item #2.

He squinted. "Your form was"—he peered closer—"exhausting."

I jabbed the parchment with my finger.

He looked again. "Oh! I mean, exhaustingly *excellent.*" He looked up. "And that's true, too. You looked bang on a proper jouster every inch of the way. Even when you toppled from Darnell there at the end, your arms flowed with—"

I elbowed him.

He swallowed. "Sorry," he mumbled. "Got carried away."

I glanced down at #3. "And as Sir Hugo always says, once you get the form down, the lance work is sure to follow. You just need a bit more practice."

"Practice." Ahead of us, Charming let out a heavy breath. "I've been training twice a day for weeks, following every instruction Sir Hugo gives. Still, I seldom hit the shield square. I don't need more practice. I need a boost, a lift of some sort, something to get me over that last hump. I need luck."

I looked at Ulff. He shook his head. I sighed and slid the list back into my tunic.

The three of us clanked past the kitchens and wound through passageways until we reached the castle library. Charming lifted the latch, and the great oak door groaned open. Charming took a breath, and we stepped inside.

It was an enormous room of dark wood and heavy

tapestries. Shelves surrounded us on all sides stretching from the thick rugs of the floor to the black shadows of the ceiling far above. Specks of dust hung in the scant light slanting through the high-set windows, and the earthy scent of old books prickled my nose. I buried my face in my hands to catch a bone-rattling sneeze.

As I wiped my sleeve across my nose, Charming marched to the center of the library and the castle's lost and found. He halted before it—a tangle of left-behind boots and bags, aprons and eyeglasses heaped on the library tables—and sighed.

Sir Roderick—the king's advisor, and also his cousin—had been cooking up parties and picnics at the castle for some weeks. Roderick said it was to get the castle staff in fit form for the upcoming jubilee. The castle staff, vexed, said their form was fine and Sir Roderick was simply trying to distract the king from Roderick's own blunders.

The staff had the right of it. After his recent fiasco with a visiting prince, a near-tragic frog spell, and Angelica's harrowing and narrowly thwarted betrothal, Sir Roderick would do anything to slither back into the king's good graces.

But many parties meant many left-behind

belongings. And since the king had not long ago put Charming in charge of castle operations, the prince was responsible for all of it. It was from the lost and found he'd plucked his lucky mitten.

Now he set the mitten on a table and gave it a pat of fond farewell.

"You served me well, noble mitten," he said.

Ulff leaned toward me. "I wouldn't say that's entirely true," he murmured.

I nodded. None of Charming's good luck charms brought him much luck. In truth, he seemed to have better luck once the charm went missing. But that didn't stop him from looking for a better one.

His gaze moved across the jumble of the lost and found, from table to table to shelf to shelf to a pair of sturdy chairs—

—until it landed at last on an enormous and ancient gold cup. This was no lost item. This was a cup placed squarely where it was meant to be, on the carved and gleaming pedestal that stood like a sentry at the far end of the library. A ray of morning sun slanted through a high library window, washing both cup and pedestal in a golden glow.

The cup was the tournament trophy, won by

Charming's father, his father's father, his father before him, and many fathers before that. Charming let his gaze slide over it.

Then over the long line of heavy-framed paintings hanging on the wall behind it. They were each of them portraits of the prince's ancestors astride noble steeds, fiercely wielding lances. Charming's gaze reached the last painting, of his own father, the king. He studied it for a long moment and blew out a soft breath.

Then he turned to the lost items piled on the nearest table—

—and the honking and hissing beneath it.

He crouched down.

"A goose," he said, "in the lost and found?" He reached out an armored hand to her. "Who leaves a goose behind after a party?"

"Who *brings* a goose to a party?" said Ulff.

I shrugged. "Maybe the door was left open and she simply wandered in from the woods."

Ulff nodded. "We've many times found wildlife in the castle. Badgers. Possums. Squirrels. Those poor, frightened piglets what locked themselves in the laundry when their house blew down."

"Yes." Charming stroked the goose's head. "But in this case, I think not."

He reached for her wing and gently fanned out the feathers.

15

"See there." He pointed to the squared-off tips. "Her wings have been clipped to stop her taking flight. She belongs to someone."

I frowned. "Someone who can't remember where they left her?"

Ulff shook his head. "That's no way to treat a goose."

"It's certainly not," said the prince.

He plucked a few wheat kernels from a strand of straw still stuck in his visor. He held them in his armored hand for the bird. She gave them a sideways glance, poked at them with her bill, then leaned in and gobbled them up.

When she finished, Charming brushed his palms together and straightened to face the lost and found. He rolled his shoulders, shook out his arms, took a fortifying breath, and dove in. He rummaged through eyeglasses and boot strings, handbags, scarves, hair ribbons, old keys, and a mustache comb, casting each one aside as unsuitably lucky.

At last, he pulled out a battered felt cap.

He held it up. "What say you? Luckier than the mitten?"

Ulff scratched his head. "I'd say most anything is luckier than a lost mitten." He shrugged. "Can't hurt to try it."

"Well said." Charming stuffed as much of the cap

into his gauntlet as would go.

He quickly tidied the mess he'd made, then turned to leave.

"With this cap in my gauntlet, I feel certain—" He paused to pinch his new good luck cap. And stopped. "Flipping flapjacks! I've lost it already."

He held up his gauntlet where he had just stuffed the cap. It was empty.

"It must be here somewhere." Charming scrabbled through the lost and found, tossing bags and boot strings this way and that.

But he couldn't find the cap.

Finally, with a long sigh, he snatched a shoestring, a hair ribbon, and the mustache comb from the pile. He stuffed all three in his gauntlet, the comb rattling against metal.

"Three charms are better than one," he said. "And this way, if one falls out, I'll still have the other two. I'm only surprised I didn't think of this sooner." He glanced at the sun now slanting higher through the library windows. "It's nearly time for the royal proclamation. To the village!"

As we trooped from the library, I heard a low, gabbling honk. I turned to find the goose waddling after us.

3

A Parade Through Twigg

Flags flew. Trumpets blared. The royal procession
rolled into Twigg.

A line of the king's trumpeters led the way, followed
by the king's men in crisp formation, each bearing the
king's royal banner on a pole above his head. Villagers
spilled from shops and houses, cheering and clapping as
they followed us up the lane.

Charming rode tall astride Darnell. His armor
gleamed in the noonday sun. His still-squashed plume
bobbed above him at a jaunty angle. And tucked before
him in the saddle . . .

. . . sat the goose.

She'd followed us as the procession left the castle,

honking and flapping to keep up until Charming, worried she'd be trampled underfoot, plucked her from the roadway. He'd let out a grunt as he lifted her to his lap.

"Blessed biscuits!" he'd said. "That's one goose heavier than she looks."

Now she sat contentedly in the saddle before him, neck stretched high while she gazed from side to side, as if she were the queen and the whole parade had been thrown in her honor.

Angelica, mounted on Rounders, rode beside them. Ulff and I scuffed along on foot, dodging plops of dung the horses had left behind.

Following us, colors fluttering, flanked by footmen, and pulled by a team of matched horses, came the king in his grand coach.

And bringing up the rear, in a small carriage that rattled and swayed over the cobblestones, was Sir Roderick.

As the procession wound its way through Twigg, I marveled at how different it was to march with royalty than to skulk through alleyways, as I'd had to do before the prince took me in, back when I was but the dung farmer's son.

I glanced about.

And frowned.

The village seemed . . . shabbier than the last time I'd been here. The shop signs sagged a bit. The blacksmith's forge clanked with less bustle. The shoemaker's, dressmaker's, and lacemaker's windows seemed skimpy with wares.

I felt for the coin pouch I kept tucked under my tunic. I'd earned a few coins in my many months assisting the prince. For the first time, I had true money to spend in the village.

But now, it seemed, the village had little for me to spend it on.

Or maybe it had always been so. I shook my head. Maybe it was my own eye that had changed, surrounded as I was each day now by finery. Maybe, with such gilt-edged pageantry parading up its lanes, the village couldn't help but look shabby.

The procession lumbered to a halt in the village square. A footman climbed from the king's coach, straightened to attention with a snap of his heel, and pulled open the coach door. His majesty, robes flowing, stepped out.

"Huzzah!" the crowd cheered.

The town crier strode forward and, with a blast of his trumpet, unfurled a scroll.

The crowd hushed.

"Hear ye! Hear ye!" the crier cried into the sudden silence. "In honor of the king's royal jubilee, his majesty the king invites all citizens of Twigg and the surrounding countryside to the jubilee's opening night ball, three days hence."

"HUZZAH!"

The crowd cheered again, louder this time, and the king's men began handing out squares of parchment—invitations to the ball. The miller's daughter hurried to take one. As did the Woodcutters. And the dressmaker, the lacemaker, and the shoemaker's wife.

His Majesty the King
invites you to be his guest at a

Masquerade Ball

three days hence in the
Grand Ballroom of the
Royal Palace

Rumpelstiltskin jangled through the crowd in his peddler's cart, pots and spoons and bits and bobs swaying. He halted his bone-weary mule near one of the king's men, leaned down from the cart seat, and snatched an invitation for himself.

The king's man snatched it back.

For the crier may have cried that all citizens of Twigg were invited, but Mr. Stiltskin was one exception. The king had banned the peddler from entering the castle after he was caught thieving from the kitchens during the last royal garden party.

Mr. Stiltskin, eyes blazing, slumped back onto his cart seat. But as he raised the reins to spur his mule forward, he spied the goose.

And stopped cold dead, hands gripped on the reins, mouth open.

I couldn't blame him. It *was* an odd sight—a goose on horseback. And it must've rankled, knowing the goose was welcome in the castle while Stiltskin himself was not.

He shook his reins, shook them again, shook a third time, and at last, the mule took an unwilling step toward Charming. But as the peddler came near, the goose hissed and raised her wings. Stiltskin flinched back in his seat.

"She's a better judge of character than I would have

thought in a barnyard bird," I whispered.

Ulff nodded.

Stiltskin, eyes narrowed, darted his gaze about the village square. He caught sight of the miller's daughter, gave the reins another shake, and jangled off after her.

Ulff shook his head. "Weaseling his way into being her ball guest, most like," he muttered.

We turned back to the prince—

—and were both of us nearly bowled flat by a robust woman in a fine-made dress. She steamed past, dragging two young women along with her. As we scrambled from out of their path, we nearly backed into their scullery maid, who scuffled behind, carrying their parasols.

The fine-dressed woman sashayed up to the king, invitation in hand.

"Your majesty." She sank into a low curtsy, then shot sharp looks at the two young women until they crouched into awkward curtsies as well. "May I present my daughters, Gert"—she waved a hand toward the tall, sturdy girl—"and Elfrida"—and toward the smaller one who seemed all nose and elbows.

The king dipped his head. "How very nice to meet you."

The woman let out a tinkly laugh. "The only surprise is that your majesty hasn't met them before." She leaned her weight on the smaller daughter, Elfrida, and struggled up from her curtsy. "Our families being so close all these years."

The king flicked an eyebrow. "Yes," he said.

"*Mother*," hissed the sturdy daughter, Gert. "Ask him about my cloak."

"Not now," the woman hissed back through clenched teeth. She beamed a smile at the king. "I daresay we'll be seeing quite a bit of each other at the upcoming festivities. I *knew* we'd receive an invitation. I told my girls as much."

"Yes, well," said the king. "You are of course invited, as is the whole of the village."

"*Mother*," whispered Gert. "My *cloak*. Tell him I left it at the castle. During the garden party."

Her mother batted her away. "We simply wanted to thank you in person, your majesty. But as lovely as it's been to chat, we must take our leave. We have a ball to prepare for, you know." She let out another twitter of laughter, gave another curtsy, and dragged her daughters off down the lane, fluttering a wave over her shoulder. Their maid followed.

As they traipsed away, Gert still mumbling about her cloak, I saw the maid quietly pluck an invitation from one of the king's men. She threw a glance toward the well-dressed woman—to make sure she wasn't seen, no doubt—then tucked it in her skirts.

Once they were gone, the king shook his head.

"That," he told Charming, "was the Widow Hedwig."

Charming frowned. "The old squire's widow?"

The king nodded. "His first wife—who sadly died quite young—was a great friend of your mother."

"My mother?" said Charming. "Truly?" He looked after the woman and her daughters with new interest.

As did I. Stiltskin, it seemed, had found little luck with the miller's daughter and was now following the Widow Hedwig and her daughters down the lane.

"And what of *this* wife?" Charming asked his father. "The second one, his widow?"

The king shook his head. "She hasn't been a friend to anyone since she arrived in Twigg. And now that the old squire is gone, she makes even less of an attempt."

Charming considered this. "Still, she stays here. I suppose she must have inherited the squire's big house and all his riches?"

The king frowned. "I seem to recall the squire had a daughter—Isabella? Petronella? Some such as that. I thought *she* was to be the squire's heir. She wasn't more than a babe when her mother died."

"Much like me," said Charming.

The king gave him a long, thoughtful look. "Yes."

"What happened to her? The daughter?" said Charming.

The king shook his head. "She was young still when the old squire died. Word came she was sent to live with relatives in a far-off kingdom. To be raised by those who loved her best, or so said the widow."

The king turned to climb back into his carriage. Then stopped, noticing the goose for the first time.

He frowned. "Please tell me that isn't your latest good luck charm."

Charming followed the king's gaze. "The goose? Oh—no! She's simply . . . I'm not sure what she is."

The goose let out a disgusted gabble.

"But I do have a new charm." The prince brightened. "Three, as it happens. One can never have too much luck."

He rummaged in one gauntlet first, then the other. Then the other again.

Then sighed.

"I had charms," he said, "but any luck they might have had seems to have worn off, since it appears I've lost all three." He looked at the goose. "I suppose she *must* be my good luck charm as she's all I have left."

The king pinched the bridge of his nose. "When we return to the castle," he said, "see me in my study."

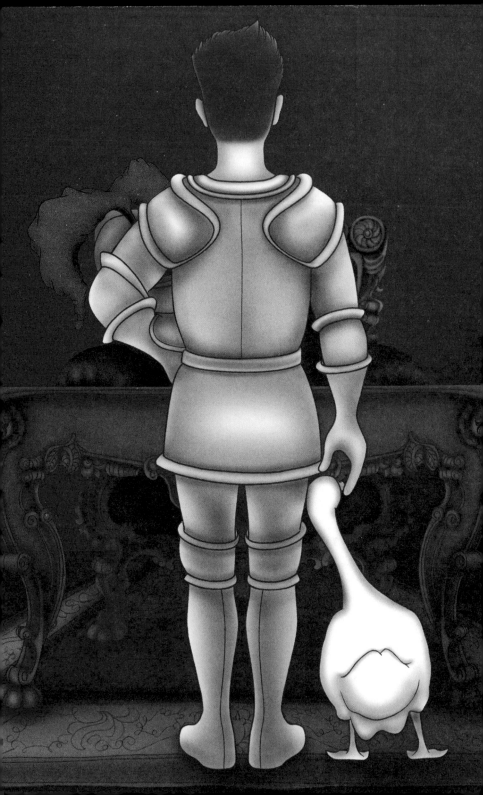

4

A Gift from the King

Charming stood before his father's desk, the tips of his armored fingers pressed against the desktop.

Bracing himself, most likely, for his father's wrath.

Or worse—his father's disappointment.

Ulff and I had backed up against a tapestry on the far wall, trying our best to be supportive. And also invisible. Ulff mopped his forehead with the back of his hand. I pulled at the neck of my tunic to give me more air. From worry or from the closeness of the room, I couldn't say. One of the maids had stirred a crackling fire, and the heat of it filled the king's small study.

The goose was there, too.

Charming had first thought to leave her in the stable

with a bucket of feed, then in the library where we'd found her. But she honked and flapped and refused to stay, and no amount of corn would convince her.

She stood guard now at the prince's side, hissing at anyone who came near. Charming gave her head an absentminded rub.

The latch on the great wooden door rattled. Ulff gulped. I stiffened. Charming clenched the edge of the desktop with his armored hands. The door swung wide and a footman stepped into the study.

"His majesty, the king," the footman called out.

Charming's father entered the room, all knotted brow and sweeping robes, sending a flutter of a breeze through the overwarm room. He spied the goose straightaway and let out a heavy sigh as he settled into his great chair. The footman swung shut the door behind him.

"Father," Charming began before his father could say anything. "I know I shouldn't need a good luck charm. You're right on that count. I shouldn't need luck at all. It's silly. I should rely on my own—"

The king raised a hand. "It's not silly."

Charming blinked. "It's not?"

Ulff and I looked at each other.

"It's not?" Ulff murmured.

The king shook his head. "It's not."

He slid open a drawer in his great desk and pulled from it a small gold box.

"The luck isn't in the charm itself," he said. "It's in what the charm means to you." He set the box on the desktop in front of him and rested his palms on its lid. "I wasn't much older than you when I entered the tournament for my own father's jubilee."

"And won," said Charming.

"Yes." The king studied the box for a moment, then opened the lid. "I carried this with me in my gauntlet."

He gently pulled out a bit of cloth trimmed in lace. He unfolded it. It was a small square of delicate fabric embroidered with the king's royal crest.

"A handkerchief." Charming stared. "It's lovely."

"Your mother made it," said the king.

Charming looked up. "My mother?"

The king nodded. "She said it would bring me luck in the tournament."

Charming's eyes grew wide. "And it did!"

"But the luck wasn't in the cloth or bits of thread. They only served to remind me that your mother believed I had the skill and courage to win. That was the luck." He held the handkerchief out to Charming. "I'm passing it on to you."

Charming stared at it, then at his father. "Truly?"

"Truly," said the king. "To remind you that you, too, have the skill and courage."

Charming took the handkerchief. He held it to his breastplate for a moment. Then he folded it into a neat square and, with great care, tucked it into the cuff of his gauntlet.

He looked up. "Thank you, Father. You shan't be disappointed."

"I have every faith in you," said the king. He eyed the goose. "So, you won't need the bird now."

The goose let out a hiss and pressed her long neck protectively against the prince's armored leg.

Charming sighed. "I fear she won't go willingly."

Ulff nodded. "Seems she's a goose in love."

5

A Goose Underhoof

Charming strode toward the tiltyard, a new *clang* in his step.

Ulff and I scuttled over the gravel of the courtyard to catch up.

The goose dawdled after us.

Charming threw a glance back, saw her skidding and skittering over the pebbles, and stopped short.

"Zooks!" he cried. "In my haste to try my new luck, I gave scant heed to small webbed feet. Apologies, dear Marge."

". . . Marge?" I said.

I looked at Ulff, who shrugged.

"I can't very well keep calling her 'the goose.'"

Charming bent down to her. "Anymore than I can call you 'the assistant' or Ulff 'the guard.' It's rude."

He looped an arm around Marge and, with a grunt, lifted her to his chest.

"Sweet griddle cakes, but you're a hefty bird," he said.

He tucked her to his breastplate, gave her neck a comforting scratch, and set out once more for the stables. Ulff and I scrambled behind.

The prince had sent a footman running ahead of us, so as we crunched up to the tiltyard, Sir Hugo was ready. He led Darnell from the stables, saddled and bridled.

In the full noonday sun, the morning's shadows had slipped back into their hiding places. The wisps of fog had vanished. Charming nestled Marge into the sun-warmed straw and, after making sure the handkerchief was still tucked in his cuff, took Darnell's reins.

I swallowed. Ulff blew out a breath. This was the tricky part—heaving Charming into the saddle and keeping him there, making sure he faced mane, not tail.

We took our positions, Ulff on one side to give the prince a boost, me on the other to stop him from sliding off onto his head.

The prince placed one armored foot into the stirrup, swung his other leg over—

—and swiftly settled into the saddle, steady and true. I kept my hands up, braced to stop him if he started to topple.

But he simply gave his tongue a click and walked Darnell to the edge of the list.

I gaped. Ulff gawked. The two of us stared at each other in wonder.

Sir Hugo trotted to the center of the tiltyard. He held up the starting flag for a moment before dropping it. Charming took a breath, squared his shoulders, and gave the hanky another pinch. Then he spurred Darnell to action, and horse and prince thundered down the tiltyard, Charming leaning forward in his saddle with more zeal and passion than I'd ever seen in him.

I was so caught up in watching the prince, I saw nothing amiss until Ulff jabbed me—hard—with his elbow.

"Ow!" I frowned and started to rub the jabbed spot.

But Ulff gave a strangled cry, grabbed my shoulder, and pointed.

At Marge.

Honking and harrumphing, she had waddled onto

the list, directly in Darnell's path. In but a split second, she would be trampled underhoof.

I sucked in a breath and opened my mouth, thinking to shout, *"Ho! Hark! Halt!"*

But before I could croak out the words, the prince flipped his lance under his arm, slid sideways in his saddle, reached with one hand, and swooped up the goose from the pathway—

—without dropping his lance.

As I stood watching, my throat burning with the breath I'd not thought to let out, the prince righted himself in the saddle.

I sagged in relief . . . until Ulff jabbed me again.

I looked up. Darnell was still charging full bore toward the quintain—

—and Marge, grasped tight to Charming's breastplate, was perched in the exact spot to take the direct hit.

I opened my mouth again. But as a choked cry rasped from my throat, Charming flipped his lance from under his arm, caught it in midair with one armored hand, and thrust it forward.

Claaaaaaang!

The tip of the lance hit the quintain's shield square.

The wooden knight swung back. The sandbag spun around—

—and whiffed through empty space.

Charming and Darnell—and Marge—had thundered safely past to the end of the tiltyard.

Ulff threw his arms in the air.

Sir Hugo whooped. "Well done, your highness!"

I stood, mouth open.

I'd never before witnessed such confidence in our prince.

Such skill.

Such agility.

Such complete lack of last-minute blunder.

I shook my head. Who knew a bit of cloth and lace could wield such power?

6

A Maiden in a Mask

Charming, Ulff, and I slipped in through a side door from the kitchens.

And were nearly blown back by glitter and noise.

Light shimmered from the chandeliers and mirrors. The *boom-tra-la* of a waltz rose and fell as partygoers twirled past in a whirl of ruffled skirts, tidy waistcoats, and elaborate ball masks. Footmen threaded their way through the guests, carrying gleaming trays of nibbles, and the scent of wood polish and ladies' perfume—with a hint of gingerbread—billowed through the air.

We had arrived at the king's jubilee ball, and we stood for a moment, taking it in. Like the other guests, Charming, Ulff, and I wore masks to disguise ourselves.

"Though I don't think we're fooling anybody," Ulff muttered. "Not many folks rattle around in spit-shined armor with two short fellows traipsing behind."

"And a goose," I said.

For Marge was with us. Charming had made her a cozy nest in a basket in his bedchamber. She roosted happily there . . . until the prince turned to leave for the ball. Then she flapped from the basket and waddled after him. He gathered her up, settled her back in her basket, and turned to leave again. She flapped out, gabbling in protest, and waddled after him. Gather, settle, turn. Flap, gabble, waddle.

They did this a few more times as Ulff and I waited. At last, near exhausted and already late for the ball, the prince slipped a tiny party mask over Marge's eyes and let her tag along.

We'd meant to steal into the ball unnoticed, but the moment we stepped into the ballroom, the king's sharp eye picked us out.

His majesty was seated in his great throne on the raised platform at the far end of the ballroom. He seemed to have a great throne in nearly every room of the castle, I'd noticed, and the same lions were carved on this one as appeared on his coat of arms.

He flicked a look at the grand ballroom clock, then at the goose, then at Charming. And even from across the room and with a mask to cloak his eyes, I couldn't miss the disappointed shake of his head.

But Charming simply gave his father a wide smile, pointed to the lace edge of the hanky peeking from his gauntlet, puffed out his armored chest, and set off across the ballroom. Marge waddled behind.

Ulff and I hurried after them, positioning ourselves on either side of the prince. A runner of carpet ran the length of the room, and in my many months at the castle,

I'd never once seen Charming cross a carpet without tripping over its edge. Ulff and I readied ourselves to catch him at the first hint of a wobble so we could right him on his feet.

But Charming deftly strode over the carpet, climbed the steps to the platform—two at a time—and took his seat beside his father. Marge settled in beside him. The prince pushed the hanky firmly back into the gauntlet and gave the bird's head a scratch.

Ulff blinked.

I shook my head in wonder. Then darted a sneak glance at the king. *His* chest, too, seemed to puff, and his disappointment melted into an understanding smile. I blew out the breath I'd been holding.

Then my sneak glance lighted on what looked to be Sir Roderick, cowering behind the king's throne. I quickly glanced away.

For it *was* Sir Roderick. Even with that barest of glances, even with him half hidden behind a drapery, even with his face disguised, there was no mistaking the black glower that seeped out from behind his mask. It near burned my back as I turned from him.

Ulff and I took our spots at the side of the platform. Ulff snagged a goblet of punch and plate of gingerbread from a passing footman and handed me a gingerbread man. As I bit off a leg, I glanced about to see who else I could pick out in the crowd.

Princess Angelica was easy to spot. She sprawled on the grand stairway, feathered mask pushed up on her forehead, cards splayed in her hands. Thistlewick, the castle butler, stood straight as a flagpole beside her. He kept one eye on the footmen in his charge, the other on the playing cards in his own hand. Angelica had clearly talked him into her favorite: a game of piquet.

But I recognized few others, likely because I was little used to seeing the villagers in fine clothes. I sniffed. I was pretty sure my father and brothers weren't there. It would take more than a mask to disguise the stench of the dung pit.

As I gazed about, I spied a young maiden entering the ballroom. She handed her invitation to the king's man at the door, then slipped quietly inside—unlike other guests, who paraded in proudly for all to see.

The maiden was clearly trying not to draw attention, but in her sparkling shoes, lace wrap, and fine sapphire gown, she could hardly hide, even behind a mask. As she circled the ballroom, her gown floated about her like a shimmering cloud.

One group of guests turned for a better glimpse of her. Then another.

And another.

Until the entire ballroom, it seemed, had turned to stare.

At first the maiden scarce noticed. But when she looked up—and saw everyone looking back—a pink blush crept up her neck and across her face, disappearing under her mask. She glanced about wildly, and her glance latched onto the platform—

—and the prince, it seemed.

She pressed a gloved hand to her mouth and took one clicking step forward, and another, headed straight for the carpet runner.

Charming, keenly aware of the peril of the carpet,

shot from his seat and down the platform. By the time the toe of the maiden's shoe caught the carpet's curled edge, he was across the ballroom.

Her toe stuck, and she pitched forward, arms flying, nothing to stop her from tumbling headlong to the polished marble floor.

Except Charming.

He swept in and—much like he'd rescued Marge on the tiltyard—caught the maiden mid-tumble. He pulled her to her feet and stepped back, hands clasped on her shoulders to steady her swaying.

The crowd went silent. Then began to clap, the claps swelling to rousing applause.

Ulff leaned toward me. "That's some fine gallantry right there," he murmured. "The maiden'll fall in love with our prince as quick as she fell over his carpet."

But the maiden took little notice of Charming. As she caught her breath and straightened her mask, she stared past the prince to the honking bird now waddling down from the king's platform.

"The goose." She blinked. "I saw the goose."

Charming frowned. "The goose? Well, yes." He turned to gaze at the bird. "You wouldn't be the first one startled to see Marge waddling about the castle, especially in a ball mask. I'd likely trip over the carpeting, too, seeing her for the first time."

The ball guests had stopped clapping, but had not stopped whispering and staring.

Charming, well used to a gawking crowd, held out his elbow to the maiden.

"If you will do me the honor of a dance," he told her, "our well-meaning partygoers will soon find something new to steal their attention."

The maiden cast a look at the crowd, swallowed, and took hold of Charming's elbow. The prince gave the hanky in his gauntlet a quick tweak for luck and led her onto the dance floor.

Ulff and I held our breaths.

"A carpet's one thing," I whispered.

Ulff nodded. "A dance floor's a whole different kettle of fish."

The prince always looked the polished dancer. Tall. Well-groomed. Excellent posture—

—until he flattened the unlucky couple behind him or mashed his poor dance partner's foot.

But this time, he glided onto the dance floor so gracefully he managed to sidestep Marge and keep the girl from tripping over a footman's foot.

The maiden eyed Marge. Marge hissed, and the maiden took a quick step back, her shoe making a distinct *clink* against the ballroom floor.

Clink?

I took a closer look at the maiden's feet.

And frowned. "Are her shoes made of . . . glass?"

Ulff leaned toward her for a squint, then nodded.

"No wonder she tripped," he said. "She can say it was Marge all she wants, but I put my wager on the shoes."

I thought it was more a mix of the two. Plus the rug. The carpets in the castle were a well-known menace.

But as I opened my mouth to say as much, a round, vaguely familiar woman seized me from behind. She wheeled me around, clutched my hand in one soft fist, my shoulder in the other, and waltzed us both onto the dance floor. She danced us so near the prince and the girl that I could hear bits of their conversation. About shoes, it seemed.

The round woman tipped her head for a better listen.

"It's true," the maiden was saying. "There's very little springiness in glass."

Aha! They *were* glass. I'd been right.

"Indeed," Charming said. "But you can't beat glass

for . . ." His voice faded as he swung the maiden in a twirl.

"For what?" hissed the round woman. "Can't beat glass for *what*?"

She thrust out her arm to steer me closer.

But in that moment, a tall, bony woman tapped her shoulder, and before I knew it, the tall woman had whisked me off, nearer the prince and the girl.

They were talking about lacy wraps now.

"It does set off your gown in good fashion," said the prince.

The maiden blushed. "I'm lucky in that. I wasn't sure *what* I'd be getting." She stopped. "I mean—one never is, are they? When putting one bit of clothing with another."

The tall woman leaned in, seeming to find the mixing and matching of ladies' garments riveting.

But I was barely listening. For I'd gotten a good look at the girl's dress. It was lovely, yes, but that wasn't what caught my eye. What caught my eye were the ribbons of one sleeve held in place with a bow, while on the other, the ribbons were fixed with a gem-crusted brooch.

I stared, not because the two sleeves were different, but because of the brooch. It was identical to a brooch

I'd found in the dung pit not long before I became the prince's assistant. I'd cleaned it up and traded it to the shoemaker for a good new pencil. At the time, I'd been quite pleased.

But now a pain of horror stabbed my chest. The gown was clearly meant to have gem-crusted brooches on both sleeves. The girl must have been to the castle a time before. She'd worn the dress, lost one of the brooches, and it had somehow ended up in the dung pit. Where I found it—

—and traded it away.

I swallowed the dry lump in my throat so lost in my thoughts, I scarce paid attention to my dancing.

Until a small, hunched woman cut in and plucked me away from the tall woman.

I blinked and shook my head.

The hunched woman swung me even nearer to the prince and maiden. They were now discussing the exact shade of the maiden's dress.

"A royal blue, would you say?"

"Perhaps. It's not dark enough to be navy."

The hunched woman spun me around, and I saw that a knobby-kneed man had snatched up Ulff and danced him close to the prince and maiden, as well.

As the prince twirled her, I heard him say, "Alas, they've all been cast into the lost and found, and I fear they'll never find their way out."

Ulff caught my eye and shook his head. I knew what he was thinking. The castle's lost and found had to be the dullest party conversation topic ever.

But the maiden seemed not to know this.

She clutched Charming's armored arm.

"You have a lost and found? Truly? Can I see it?" She swallowed. "What I mean is, perhaps I can help you sort it out."

Charming's eyes grew wide. "Help me sort—?"

He stopped dancing, held his arm out to the girl, and escorted her across the ballroom.

7

A Strike of Midnight

Marge honked and flapped behind Charming and the maiden, clearing a path through startled party guests and servants.

I peeled myself from the hunched woman, Ulff untangled himself from the knobby-kneed man, and we scrambled after them. Ulff, stomach growling from all the dancing, snatched more gingerbread and punch from a footman as we slipped out the door.

We meandered down a winding stone passageway. Charming's armor clanked. The maiden's glass slippers clinked. Marge's goose feet slapped. Ulff and I shuffled and thumped. Finally, noisily, we reached the library.

Charming pulled the latch, swept open the great oak

door, and stood back. Soft light from the library's oil lamps glowed within.

The girl darted a look at Charming, then stepped inside—

—and gasped.

She clapped both hands over her mouth as she took in the shelves and shelves and shelves that stretched from the wood-planked floor to the dark shadows of the ceiling. She took another step forward, her eyes running over the great gathering of books—

—then gasped again and stepped back.

Charming, Ulff, and I crowded in to see what was amiss. Marge pushed through our legs with her bill.

A man stood in the shadows of the shelves. He was tall, draped in black robes, and his own shadow, cast by lamplight, loomed taller and blacker still. He stood before the trophy, his back to us, gazing up at the winners' portraits.

He must have heard us. We were not a quiet bunch. But he stood there for another moment before turning. The eyes behind his mask were as black as his robes, and as his look settled on us in the doorway, his mouth twisted into a scowl.

"Sir Roderick," said Charming.

Marge let out a low sound, more of a growl than a hiss.

Ulff and I shot glances at each other. I thought we'd left Sir Roderick behind in the ballroom, but he must have slipped out while we were dancing.

He gave a small bow. "Pardon me, your *highness*," he said with snarling politeness. "I had no idea you would be entertaining in the library this eve. Did you come to show this lovely girl where you hope *your* portrait will hang?"

"I—well, no," said Charming. "Of course not." He lifted his chin. "I've come to show her the lost and found."

"Really?" Sir Roderick tossed a glance at the mountain of lost objects. "She'll no doubt be impressed." His mustache twitched. "I'll bid farewell then and leave you to it."

He bowed again and strode toward the door. Marge nipped at his robes. Ulff and I scrambled aside to let him through.

As he brushed Marge away, he flicked a finger against the corner of the hanky peeking from the prince's gauntlet.

"I see your father has tried to give you some luck," he

told Charming. His mustache twisted again. "I imagine you'll need it."

He stepped through the door and was gone, seeming to suck the very air out of the room with him.

"Yes, well," Charming said after a moment. "That was my father's, uh—"

"Knave? Wretch? Snake-breath swine?" Ulff suggested.

"—cousin," said Charming finally. He turned. "And here, as promised, is the lost and found."

He waved an arm toward the mountain of castoffs.

And the maiden gasped for a third time.

Then went to work.

She picked up a buckled leather shoe between her thumb and finger and held it away from her. She leaned toward the pile it had come from, peering this way and that.

"Can I help you . . . find something?" said Charming.

"The mate," said the maiden.

"The mate?" Charming frowned.

"Yes." She tipped her head toward the shoe in her hand. "Do none of these castoffs have mates?"

"Alas, no." Charming placed his hands on his hips and surveyed the pile. "I mean, I presume they have

60

mates somewhere, but none here in the library. When castle guests leave belongings behind, they rarely leave them in pairs. Mittens, stockings, boots, knitting needles"—he shook his head—"it's always just the one."

The maiden nodded. She took a step toward the nearest pile and circled it, head tipped, as if looking for an angle of attack. She seemed to find it in the dangling edge of a cape. She dove in, pulling out the cape, then a purse, then a headscarf, until she was flying through the mountain of lost things, sorting, folding, grouping, and arranging.

Charming watched, mouth open, eyebrows raised high above his ball mask.

"She's the most organized person I've ever seen," I whispered.

The prince nodded, spellbound.

The maiden plucked up each item with passion, turning it upside down and inside out and giving it a shake before letting out a small sigh and placing it in its proper pile.

She was a whirlwind, and the billow of dust she stirred up had me pinching my nose to stop from sneezing. Charming stretched a hand toward the heap to help, but was slapped across the face by a flying pair of hosen. He pulled back his hand.

"It's almost a danger to be near her," Ulff whispered.

Marge, standing protectively before the prince, edged closer to the table, poking her bill in and among the piles of lost and found.

The maiden spied the goose and stopped in the midst of folding a bonnet. She chewed her lip and studied the goose, then reached into her skirts and pulled out a handful of beans. They were strange-looking. Large, misshapen, and colored with a tinge of—I peered closer—blue? When the maiden held them out to Marge, the goose hissed, clamped shut her bill, and turned her head away.

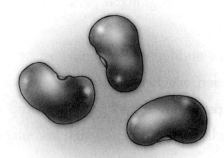

"Odd that." The prince frowned. "She usually loves nothing more than a crunchy snack."

The maiden took a breath, as if to steel herself, and thrust the beans closer. Marge hissed again and raised her wings, flapping them against the lost and found. A cloak tumbled from the pile and landed with a *thunk* on the library floor. A book bounced from its pocket.

"There!" The maiden bent to pick it up.

But Marge, with a startled honk, reached it first. She wrenched the book away and set onto it, nipping and gnawing.

"No!" The maiden let out a cry.

Charming leaned down to tug the book away. Marge tugged back. The cover began to tear.

"Vexation." The prince sighed. "I'll need to have it repaired before I can even think to find its rightful owner."

"I'll do it!" the maiden blurted. Then swallowed. "I mean, your highness shouldn't have to worry about such trivial things. I would consider it an honor to repair the book—*and* find its owner."

But Charming, still tugging at the book, waved a hand. "I can't burden you with this. It's entirely my responsibility. I'll have Thistlewick take care of it."

He gave one more tug, and the book broke free.

Marge let out a honk and a flap, thumping a wing against Ulff's elbow. A gingerbread man bounced from the plate. As Ulff lunged to catch it, his goblet tipped, splashing punch right down the girl's shimmering blue gown.

"Oh!" cried the maiden. She stared down at her punch-drenched dress.

"Apologies," moaned Ulff. He stared down at his empty goblet.

Charming thrust a cloth at the maiden. "You must get it out before it stains."

The maiden took the cloth. But as she began dabbing at the punch, an enormous *BONNGGG!* rang through the castle.

It was the great clock in the ballroom.

Striking the first chime of midnight.

The girl looked up, eyes wide.

She glanced at the door.

Then at Charming

Then at the goose.

BONNGGG!

The clock chimed again.

The maiden closed her eyes, gave a small shake of her head—

—and bolted from the library.

Charming shot an alarmed look at Ulff and me and raced after her. Ulff and I followed, with Marge raising her wings and flapping after us, nearly knocking down the round woman, the tall woman, the hunched woman, and the knobby-kneed man lurking just outside the door—as was, strangely, Sir Roderick.

Charming ran headlong into Roderick with a *clang*, bouncing them both back a bit.

"Forgive me!" Charming cried out as he quickly recovered and raced off.

Ulff and I edged our way around Roderick and followed. Marge flapped on our heels.

BONNGGG!

We wound through the passageway, dodged our way across the ballroom, and raced out the great castle doors into the moonlight.

But the maiden was gone.

All that was left of her was one shimmering glass shoe lying by itself at the bottom of the steps.

8

A Clue in the Shoe

Charming scooped up the shoe. He brushed a bit of gravel from the toe and glanced about the moonlit courtyard.

"Hello!" he called. "Miss, uh . . . young maiden! Are you there?" He took a step toward the shadows of the guardhouse. "Somewhere?" He turned and called toward the stables. "You've lost your shoe."

He stood still for a moment. We all did, even Marge, heads tipped, listening.

All we heard was the low croak of a bullfrog in the garden pond and a stiff wind snapping the king's flags high on the turrets. And in the distance, a faint jangle. I frowned. The jangle reminded me of something, but

I couldn't think what. I listened, but the jangle did not come again.

Charming sighed. He held up the shoe and gave it a long look. Moonlight filled the glass, giving the slipper a magical glow.

"She was such help with the lost and found," he said. "And now . . ."

He shook his head.

He reached into his gauntlet to pinch the hanky—

—and let out a strangled cry.

He dug in the gauntlet, then the other, then took them both off, peered inside, held them upside down, gave them a shake—

—and found nothing.

He looked up, face white.

"The handkerchief." His voice was a rasp, like the crinkle of old paper. "My mother made it. My father entrusted it to me." He swallowed. "And I've lost it."

Ulff frowned. "Can't be *too* lost," he said. "It has to be here at the castle."

I nodded. "You haven't gone anywhere else."

Charming brightened. "Of course. It *must* be here." He set off up the stairway. Then stopped. "But where?"

I let out a breath. "Where do you last remember having it?" I said.

The prince frowned. "Let me think. I had it when I was jousting." He counted off on his fingers. "And when I was getting dressed for the ball. I had it just before I entered the ballroom, and while I was dancing."

"What about the library?" I said.

"The library!" Charming held up an armored finger. "*That's* the last place I remember having it."

He set off once more. Ulff, Marge, and I scrabbled up the steps after him.

"I remember having it as I watched that industrious young maiden burrow through the lost things—she really was remarkable; I've never seen the lost and found so tidy—because I noticed a lacy corner hanging out. So I reached down, gently took hold of it, and was about to tuck it back in when"—he frowned—"I heard a great squawking—"

"That was me." Ulff nodded.

"—and a gasp—"

"That was me, too," said Ulff.

"I looked up, and there was the girl with punch all down her dress—"

"Me again." Ulff gave a sad shake of his head.

"—so immediately I—"

Charming looked up, eyes wide.

"Grandad's girdle," he whispered. He sank down on

69

the top step, his face whiter than before. "I thrust a bit of cloth into the maiden's hand so she could mop the punch from her gown."

I stared at him.

Ulff gulped. "The hanky?"

"It must have been." Charming dropped his head into his hands. "Now she's gone, the hanky with her, and I have no way to find her. I never even asked her name."

"You have her shoe," I pointed out.

"Yes." Charming gave it a sideways glance. "I'll need to find a place for it in the library." He sighed. "One more lost thing."

"Or," I said, "one big shiny found thing. A clue!"

Charming looked up, puzzled.

Ulff nodded.

"You find the girl what lost the shoe," he said, "you find the hanky."

9

A Question for the Village

$\mathfrak{E}$arly the next morning, we set off for Twigg.

Workers had begun building the tournament arena in the meadow beyond the castle. The steady bang of hammers and scrape of saws followed us down the hill.

The sun shone warm on our faces and gleamed off Charming's breastplate—puffed high now with confidence—while a brisk breeze fluffed the squashiness from his plume. Darnell trotted along with a jaunt in his step, and Ulff with a bounce in his boots. I felt an extra spring in my own feet as I closed my eyes and breathed in the scent of freshly cut hay in the king's fields. The day was new, and hope seemed to fill the very air. Even the birds in the trees seemed to chitter an optimistic chirp.

Ulff reached into his tunic. We'd stopped first at the butler's pantry to leave the goose-chewed book for Thistlewick to repair. As we left, Cook had handed Ulff a kitchen towel filled with gingerbread. Now he pulled it out.

"What's our plan for the shoe?" he asked.

He picked out a gingerbread man and took a bite of its head. He held the towel out to me. I took a gingerbread man frosted in blue.

"We'll simply ask the villagers if they know who dropped it," said Charming. "We'll have the hanky back anon."

I cast a sideways look at Ulff. He stopped mid-chew.

"He's one fine prince," he muttered, swallowing the gingerbread. "But he scarce knows our villagers."

I took a bite of frosted gingerbread arm. I couldn't disagree.

At the bottom of the hill, we passed Swill Cottage. By its name, it half sounded charming. But it was more hovel than house, home to a family of dung farmers: my father, my brothers, and, not long ago, me.

Charming did not stop, nor even slow. He had no need. My brothers were surprisingly good dancers, but they were none of them maidens. And the stench of dung and the snores of my family—which could shake the nails from the very walls—would have warded off any stray maidens who happened by.

Beyond Swill Cottage, we came at last to Twigg. Charming turned up the same lane the royal procession had taken only a few days past. This day, we made a great deal less fuss and noise. Only the steady clop of Darnell's hooves on the cobblestones and a grumbling honk from Marge announced our arrival.

But Twigg folk let nothing pass their notice. By the time Charming halted in the village square, a crowd had already gathered— nearly everyone from the village, plus a few folk I didn't recognize. A boy and his cow. A young girl who'd dragged a tuffet along with her for some reason. A small old man in a bulky, hooded cloak who seemed particularly interested in Marge. He limped closer for a better look, but hobbled off again when Marge turned, wings raised, and hissed.

"What luck!" The prince, sitting tall astride Darnell,

gazed over the crowd. "With the villagers all here, we've no need to chase them down house to house."

He handed me the shoe, Ulff the goose, held the reins himself, and swung his leg around to climb down.

With my hands full, protecting the glass slipper, I could do nothing to stop him.

But Ulff, eyes wide, deposited Marge on the cobbles, thrust his gingerbread man in her bill, and straightened in time to catch the prince mid-tumble. He tipped Charming upright.

The prince adjusted his breastplate and turned to the crowd. I handed him the shoe. Ulff reached for his gingerbread, but Marge had already gulped it down.

"Good villagers of Twigg!" called the prince. He leaned down and lowered his voice. "Nobbin, take note."

I nodded. I'd already rustled a scrap of paper from my tunic. Now I smoothed it and held a pencil nub— all that was left of the sturdy pencil I'd traded the shoemaker for—at the ready.

"Good villagers," Charming said again. "This lovely glass slipper"—he held it up—"was left behind after the ball, and I seek to find its owner. Is anyone by chance the maiden who dropped it?"

Every villager, it seemed, thrust an arm in the air. Some thrust two. And a leg.

Charming studied the sea of waving hands and feet. His face knotted in a frown.

He turned to Ulff and me. "We need better organization."

"Perhaps we should sort them," I said. "The *aye*s from the *nay*s."

Charming nodded. "Excellent thought."

He turned back to the villagers.

"Those of you who believe the shoe is yours, step to the right side of the square." He gestured with his arm. "Those of you who harbor no claim, step to the left." He gestured again.

The villagers looked at each other, then at their hands, trying to pick the left from the right. Charming marched forward to help. With much shuffling and grumbling, a few *ouch*es, a handful of *fie*s, and one "You beef-witted clout! You stepped on my foot," the villagers sorted themselves.

Charming stepped back, straightened his helmet—which had been knocked sideways in the scuffle—and studied his work.

If the square had been a seesaw, the right side would have banged to the ground and sent the left side flying. Every villager had crowded to the right, save the witch, who stood by herself, arms crossed, on the left. She

77

gazed across the square at the jostling knot of town folk, shook her head, and turned to march back to her gingerbread cottage in the woods.

Now every last villager was on the right.

Charming's armored shoulders slumped.

"They couldn't have *all* lost shoes," he said. "And even if they had, only a scant few of them are maidens." He shook his head. "Who could've guessed our own town folk could be so wholly less than honest?"

Ulff raised his hand. I raised my pencil. Darnell snorted and swished his tail. Marge gave her own tail a shake and nipped at Ulff's leg for another piece of gingerbread.

Charming was pacing now. "Take the woman from the boot-shaped cottage." He flung a hand toward her. "She couldn't have even *been* at the ball. We would've noticed the dozens of children trailing behind her, surely. And the dwarfs. Even now, they're bickering amongst themselves about which should claim the slipper as his own. I had to stop a fistfight breaking out between the cranky one and the poor, red-nosed one with allergies. As for the rest, most of their feet don't come within a foot of fitting—"

He stopped.

His eyes grew wide.

"That's it!" he said. "We'll ask them to try it on. We'll find the foot that fits."

Ulff frowned. "But lots of people have feet the same size. Me and my sister, for two. We're always getting our boots mixed up. If we start trying that shoe on folks, we could still end up with a crowd."

"Then we'll simply find the foot that fits *best*," said Charming.

10

A Fit of the Foot

Charming faced the villagers once more.

"Fine folk of Twigg," he said. "We seem to have a bit of confusion over the ownership of the shoe. With apologies, I must ask each of you to try it on."

He borrowed the tuffet from the young girl and set it in the center of the square. We lined up the villagers—a line that circled the square twice and stretched down the lane. We had thought we'd only be fitting the shoe on village maidens. And the line was surely sprinkled with maidens. But also young men.

And children. And their parents. And grandparents. And a few people not related to anyone.

One by one, they came forward to sit on the tuffet. Charming knelt before them to test the shoe . . .

. . . on each and every right foot in the village and surrounding countryside.

Ulff kept the line going, while I sorted the villagers after their fitting. Folk who couldn't squeeze their foot into the shoe at all were the easiest. I merely sent them on their way. The others I sorted into groups, from the feet that fit best to the feet that fit with a bit of a pinch.

The sun rose high in the sky. The village square became a baking stone, the brisk breeze of the morning long gone. Ulff fanned himself with his cap. I flapped my tunic, trying to stir up a bit of cool air. Someone thought to bring an armload of hay for Darnell, and Marge settled into it for a doze, head nested on her back. Darnell nibbled at the hay around her.

Charming held out as long as he could, but finally cast aside his helmet and, after a time, his gauntlets. He'd started the morning kneeling gallantly on one knee, sliding the glass slipper onto each right foot with care and courtesy. Now he slumped cross-legged on the cobblestones and handed each villager the shoe to try on for themselves.

At last we came to the final villager—the woodcutter. He took his seat on the tuffet. Charming mopped the back of his hand across his forehead and handed him the shoe.

The woodcutter pulled up his pant leg, held his foot in the air, and slid the glass slipper over his hairy big toe. He wriggled and wiggled, pushed and squeezed, twisted one way, then another. But his toe just stuck there, like a stopper in a bottle. The shoe would slide no further.

Finally, the woodcutter popped it back off. "Just as I thought," he said. "But I had to try."

He handed the shoe to Charming, picked up his own boot, and ambled off toward his cottage.

Charming peered around the tuffet to make sure no other villagers lurked in line, then rose to his feet, armor creaking and screeching. He put a hand to his lower back and took a stretch, bones cracking, then turned to study the villagers that remained.

They were tired and sweaty and cranky and bored, lined up across the square from good fit to bad.

Ulff shook his head. "Worst beauty pageant ever," he said.

The best fit stood with his family's milk cow on the far-right side of the square. His name was Jack, and he was the boy I hadn't recognized earlier, most likely because he'd wandered through Twigg only that morning looking for a good price for his cow. His foot fit the slipper as if it were made for him.

"But *he* can't be the mysterious maiden," said Charming.

Ulff shook his head. "He's a lad."

"And he only just got to town," I said.

"And he's much too short," said Charming. "I'm certain I never danced with him."

With a heavy sigh, he dismissed them all. The villagers, mumbling and grumbling but glad to be finished with the irksome shoe at last, trudged back to their homes and shops.

When they'd gone, we saw they'd left a straggle of shoes and boots behind. They'd pulled them off their own feet to try on the slipper, and many of them had forgotten to pick them up when they left.

Ulff, hands on hips, glared at the scattered shoes. "I'm not picking that up," he said.

Charming stared, eyes wide, a glisten in his eye as if he might like to cry.

"I can't think where in the library we'll find room for it all," he said.

"I can't think we'll have to," I said. "At some point, the village folk will figure out they're limping about lopsided, realize they've only one shoe on, and come back to retrieve the other. If not"—I shrugged—"these shoes don't *have* to go in the library. They weren't lost at the castle, after all."

Charming looked at me. "They weren't, were they? Huh! If the villagers want a lost and found, they'll need to organize it for themselves."

He gave a decisive nod.

But then, because he was Charming, he sighed and said, "And when they don't, I'll send a footman down with a cart to gather the shoes."

He propped his elbows on Darnell's saddle and let his gaze slide over the empty square.

"I had such hope for our villagers," he said. "They seem always to know each other's business. I thought surely they'd know who dropped the shoe. I believed we'd simply have to ask and snip-snap, we'd have the hanky back. But we're no closer to finding it now than we were when we set out this morn."

He blew out a long, shuddering breath. Marge roused herself from the hay and waddled over to press her neck against his leg. Ulff patted his armored shoulder.

But I'd been making detailed notes. I ran my finger down them now, reading each line.

And realized we'd missed an important clue. I shook my head. How had I missed it?

"The shoe," I said. I looked up. "It's a *shoe*."

Charming studied me, eyes narrowed. "Of course

it's a *shoe*, Nobbin. That's why we've been sliding it onto *feet*."

"But *shoes*," I said, "are made by shoe*makers*."

Charming frowned. Then brightened.

"We have a shoemaker in this very village," he said.

Ulff nodded. "*And . . . ?*" he asked the prince, encouragingly.

"*And . . .*" Charming frowned, tumbling this thought in his head. He straightened and thrust a finger in the air. "*And* if we find the maker of the shoe, we'll find the foot that fits. We find the foot that fits, we'll find the hanky."

He handed the glass slipper to Ulff.

"Oof!" Ulff waved his hand before his face, trying to wave away the stink. "This thing's going to need a good scrub when we get back to the castle," he said. "With soap."

But the prince could not fret about shoe stench just then. He plucked his up helmet and gauntlets from the cobblestones and took firm hold of Darnell's reins.

"To the shoemaker's!" he said.

11

A Shoe in the Shop

The little bell over the door jingled as Charming swung it open and we clumped into the tiny shop. The scent of shoe wax and new leather folded us in a warm swirl.

"Way better smell than this." Ulff turned his head and held the glass slipper away from him.

The shoemaker's wife was running a feather duster over a row of shelves. At the sound of the bell, she glanced up.

"Oh!" She stuffed the duster in a drawer and slid it shut with her hip. She straightened her hair and skirt. "Your highness!"

I took a quick step behind Charming, out of her view. I was the prince's assistant.

I lived in the castle now.

But I hadn't forgotten the slap of Mrs. Shoemaker's broom when she used to chase me away to stop the stench of me driving off paying customers.

She craned her head toward a curtained doorway at the back of the shop.

"Albert," she called in a sweet singsong. "We have a customer."

As we waited, I glanced about. When I was but a dung farmer's son, I had the chance to visit the shoemaker's often, trading for things I found. I had skulked in from the alleyway in those days and bargained with the shoemaker in his workshop in the back.

Today was the first day I'd strolled through the front door like a proper customer.

But again I noticed that, like other shops on the lane, the shoemaker's seemed sadly barren. It was spit shined and spotless, the floors and display shelves gleaming, the window glass polished till not a streak of dirt blocked the sunlight that peeked in. Mrs. Shoemaker had surely been busy with her duster and broom.

But those gleaming displays were near empty. Only a sprinkling of shoes dotted the shelves. One pair of boots—finely made but lonely—sat on a table in the window beside a small arrangement of shoelaces.

The curtain at the back rustled open, and the shoemaker emerged, brushing threads from his leather apron.

"I was in the midst of a tricky bit of stitching, Agnes," he said. "Can you not take care of—?"

He looked up and saw Charming. And stopped short. His eyebrows leapt to his forehead.

"Oh!" He ran a hand over his head, smoothing the few hairs that remained there. "Your highness! Can I be of service?"

"Good sir, you may be the only one who can." Charming held out his hand, and Ulff placed the shoe in it.

The shoemaker's eyes grew wide. His wife pressed a hand to her throat.

"The glass slipper." The shoemaker ran an admiring gaze over it. "It's the talk of Twigg." He looked up. "But I fear you've wasted a trip, your highness. My wife and I tried on that very shoe only an hour past in the village square. We were neither of us a good fit."

"They weren't any kind of fit at all," muttered Ulff.

"Yes." The prince frowned. "I do recall you there."

He put an armored finger to his lips, trying to root out the memory.

"Ah!" He raised his finger in the air. "Your fine

91

wife's foot became quite stuck. It took three men and a goodly jar of bacon grease to wrench it free."

"Oh!" Mrs. Shoemaker let out a squeak.

Pink patches blotched her neck, and she turned to rearrange the shoelaces in the window.

"My feet," she murmured, "are unusually swollen this day from the heat."

The shoemaker nodded. Then frowned.

"But you still have the slipper," he told Charming. "Did you not find its owner?"

"Alas, no." Charming shook his head. "To that end"—he held up the shoe—"I imagine you must have made this fine piece of footwear. What I need to know is who you made it *for*."

"For?" The shoemaker gave a sad shake of his head. "I only wished I'd made it at all. It's the loveliest shoe I've ever set my eyes on."

Charming frowned, confused. "But you must have made it. Surely. You're the only shoemaker in the village."

"I am." The shoemaker sighed. "But as you can see, my shelves of wares are all but bare. I've little money to buy leather to make more. I surely couldn't afford fine crystal to craft a shoe such as that."

"So you've no thought who could have worn this shoe?" said Charming.

The shoemaker shook his head.

The prince swallowed back his disappointment. Marge gave his armored leg a sympathetic rub with her head.

"In that case"—the prince drew a breath—"we'll take our leave and allow you to return to your toil. Thank you, good sir." He tipped his head to the shoemaker, then to his wife. "Madam."

He turned and, with head bowed and feet heavy, shuffle-clanked from the shop, Ulff and Marge at his heels.

But as they jingled out the door, I stayed where I was. I patted the pouch of coins tucked under my tunic. This could be my chance to right a wrong.

I waited till the door had firmly thumped shut, then turned to the shoemaker.

He eyed me, brows raised.

I swallowed. "Do you remember a gem-crusted brooch I once brought you?" I asked.

I kept my voice quiet and darted a look at his wife. She'd gone back to her dusting, but kept her head tilted and ears perked.

"A brooch I, um, found?" I didn't want to mention I'd fished it from the dung. "I traded it to you for a pencil."

The shoemaker, too, cut a look at his wife. She never liked him bargaining for dung finds, no matter how rare.

"Gem-crusted, you say?" He swallowed. His Adam's apple bobbed. "I seem to recall such a brooch, yes."

He recalled it! Huzzah! My shoulders felt as if they'd tossed off a large stone they'd been carrying.

I leaned forward. "Do you perchance still have it?"

"Glory, no." The shoemaker waved a hand. "You've seen the state of my shop." He let his gaze run over the empty shelves. "Anything I ever had of value I've used to buy supplies."

His wife cast him a sharp look, and he lowered his voice.

"I swapped that brooch long ago for a length of shoe leather," he said.

"Oh." I nodded. "Of course."

My shoulders slumped under the weight of the rock once more. I had thought to trade a coin or two to get the brooch back. I'd wanted to return it to its rightful owner—if we ever found her.

I had but one hope left.

"Do you recall who you traded it *to*?" I asked.

The shoemaker slid a quick look at his wife once again. She watched him carefully, one eyebrow raised.

"It's of little matter," he said. "It was a lovely piece of jewelry. It would have fetched a good price. It's long gone by now."

12

A Widow in the Lane

The prince was unlooping Darnell's reins from a lamppost when I caught up to him.

We set off down the lane—

—and were nearly flattened a second time by the Widow Hedwig.

She once more had her daughters in tow. It was but the three of them this day. No scullery maid lurked behind.

"Your highness!" The widow, out of breath, clapped a hand to her chest and leaned on her smaller daughter, Elfrida, for support. "What fortune we found you! We only just heard of the glass slipper. We feared we'd missed our chance to try it."

Charming raised his eyebrows. "It was one of your daughters who lost the shoe at the ball?" he said.

"They might have," said the widow. "We won't know till we try, will we?" She tipped her head toward her stouter daughter. "Gert."

Gert bent and tugged at her own shoe till at last it wrenched free. She dropped it to the walkway, leaned against a lamppost with one hand and Elfrida's poor bony shoulder with the other, and lifted her bare foot in the air.

Charming sighed and knelt before her. He slid the slipper onto her foot.

Or tried to, leastways. Gert's foot was so wide, she could barely wedge the tips of her toes in. She twisted up and down, side to side, this way and that, with Charming gallantly clenching the shoe in both hands to stop it shattering upon the walk.

Finally, he slid the shoe off and brushed his plume back from his face.

"Alas," he said. It came out as more a gasp for air than an actual word. "Your foot is not a fit. Perhaps it's swollen. From the heat."

"There's a lot of that going around," said Ulff.

Gert leaned against the frame of the dressmaker's

window to catch her breath and pull her own shoe back on.

Elfrida slipped her right shoe off with the toe of the other and stuck out her bare foot.

Her bare, bony foot.

So bony that when Charming slipped on the slipper, it just kept slipping, until her entire foot was swallowed by shoe with acres of empty space gaping on all sides.

"Perfect!" Elfrida hiked up her skirts for a better look. "I'll just need to wear thick socks."

"Alas," Charming said again. "I'm afraid the maiden wore no socks to the ball."

He lifted Elfrida's foot from the slipper.

"She *could* have," snipped Elfrida. She snatched up her own shoe and stomped away.

Charming started to rise.

"Good madam," he said. "I fear your daughters are not—"

He looked up.

And found the widow herself dangling a bare foot before him.

He jerked back in surprise. Then quickly recovered.

"Ah, yes. Apologies," he said. "I suppose there *are* three sets of feet in your family."

He pressed the shoe onto her foot.

But it wouldn't slide past her bunion.

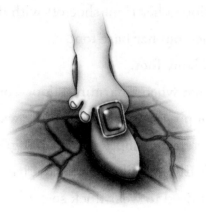

"It *must* fit." The widow gritted her teeth as she pushed. "If you're to be married, it should be to someone highborn, someone from our"—she grunted—"house."

Ulff, Darnell, and I gave each other wide-eyed looks. Marge hissed and nipped at the widow's skirts.

"Married?" Charming pulled the shoe from the widow's foot. He clutched it protectively against his armored chest. "Whyever would you think I'm to be married?"

The Widow Hedwig leaned against Elfrida, out of breath. "It's the talk of the village," she said. "It's why you're trying the shoe. To find the maiden who stole your heart."

She held up her foot once more, to Gert this time.

Who picked up her mother's shoe and squeezed it back onto her foot.

"The maiden did not steal my heart," said Charming. "She stole my hanky."

Hedwig frowned. "So you won't ask her to marry you?"

"Good gobblesmack, no," said Charming.

Elfrida shook her head. "That's going to disappoint the village."

Gert nodded.

"Though I may hire her to clean out the library," said Charming. "She's made a cracking start already."

"Clean?" Elfrida wrinkled her nose. "I'm not cleaning anything, not even the castle. That's Cinderella's job."

She and her sister and mother turned to leave.

But I looked up from the notes I'd been taking.

"Cinderella?" I asked.

Gert rolled her eyes. "Our step—"

"Scullery maid," the Widow Hedwig rushed to say.

"Step-scullery maid?" Ulff scratched his head.

"Step-scullery maid!" said Charming, visibly cheered. "We'll try the shoe on *her*!"

"Oh. No." Hedwig gave a laugh and waved the idea away. "It would be a waste of your highness's time. Our scullery maid did not attend the ball."

"Obviously," said Elfrida.

"Utterly obviously," said Gert.

"She wouldn't have had a thing to wear," Hedwig continued.

"Altogether utterly obviously," said Gert.

"Not a glass shoe, that's for sure," said Elfrida.

"Plus, she had to stay home and cook," said Gert.

Cook? I frowned. "That late at night?"

"Oh!" The widow let out a tinkly laugh. "Just a light snack. For when we returned home."

Gert nodded. "Potatoes, gravy, a leg of mutton, a roast chicken, dumplings—"

"Some snack!" said Ulff, impressed.

"—a jam tart, some sugarplums, hot cross buns, and a figgy pudding."

"Figgy?" Ulff shuddered.

I grimaced.

The prince gulped.

Our recent visiting prince had been named Figgy, and we were none of us eager to recall his stay at the castle.

Charming sighed. "I suppose there's no use trying the shoe on your maid, then. That kind of snack would have taken all day and all night to cook. She couldn't have been at the ball."

Ulff shrugged. "Didn't stop us trying the shoe on the rest of the village," he said.

"True." Charming sighed again. "Madam, lead the way."

The Widow Hedwig huffed, but seeing no way to put off the prince, led us off down the lane.

We reached her house on the far side of Twigg. It was a large affair, tall and broad with great wood timbers and gables angled in every direction.

But when the widow led us through the house to the kitchens where the maid was sure to be, we found the kitchen door swinging open.

And Cinderella gone.

13

A Maid Gone Missing

The Widow Hedwig's face turned purple to match her two quivering fists.

"Where," she spit out through clenched teeth, "can that miserable, rude, ungrateful wretch—?"

She stopped.

And darted a look at the prince.

She choked back whatever words she meant to spit out next and molded her purple scowl into what I think was supposed to be a kindly expression. She looked like she'd accidentally swallowed a bug.

"I mean, *girl*," she said, unclenching her teeth.

"Where can the poor, sweet, darling girl have gone?"

The knot of us stood bunched in the kitchen of the widow's house. It was a small, dark room, the beams of the ceiling so low, they brushed the top of Charming's squashed plume. A scarred wooden table took up the most of it, and a large stone fireplace stretched the length of the back wall, its fire long gone cold.

"What *I* want to know"—Elfrida crossed her arms, pointy elbows jutting like weapons—"is when she'll be back."

"Because *someone*"—Gert crossed her beefier arms—"needs to cook our lunch."

"And iron our clothes," said Elfrida.

"And scrape our shoes," said Gert.

"And change our sheets."

"And fluff our pillows."

"And brush our hair."

"And trim our toenails."

"Eww . . ." Ulff shuddered.

"Fear not," said Charming. "I am the royal detective. If your maid has gone missing, my men and I will find her."

He squared his shoulders, lifted his chin—

—and glanced at me.

I leaned in close. "A look through the house?" I whispered. "She may well be here somewhere."

"Quite right." He turned back to the widow. "We will search your fine house from attic to cellar. We'll not stop until we've turned up your maid."

And so we did. We combed the attic. We scoured the cellar. We rummaged the closets and crawled under beds. We rooted through cupboards. We shook the draperies. We looked up the chimney and lifted the rugs. We even traipsed outside and poked around the grounds, and Ulff shimmied under a small shed in the back.

At last we plodded back to the kitchen, where the widow and her daughters still waited. We were out of breath, covered in soot, and wheezing from dust. Ulff's clothes were caked with wet leaves and mud, and a cobweb dangled from Charming's plume.

"Alas." The prince bent over, hands on his armored knees. "Your maid is not in your house."

"Nor gardens." Ulff gasped in a breath. "We looked."

"Not to worry." Charming managed to hold up an armored finger. "We shall find out where she's gone."

I wrestled my pencil nub and a fresh scrap of paper from my dust-smudged tunic.

Charming opened his mouth. And cut a glance at me.

"Are her things gone?" I whispered.

"Excellent." He straightened. "Have you noticed whether her things are gone, as well?" he asked the Widow Hedwig.

"Things?" The widow's face rumpled in confusion. She shook her head. "What things?"

"Things such as . . . " Charming slid his eyes toward me.

"Personal things," I whispered. "And something to carry them in."

"Ah, yes." He turned to the widow. "Clothing, shoes, trinkets, perhaps a traveling bag. The sort of things you might take with you if you'd decided to leave for good."

Now Elfrida's face rumpled. "She doesn't *have* things. Only the clothes she wears each day."

I scribbled this in my notes.

"Old clothes," said Gert.

"Sooty clothes," said Elfrida.

"And the book," said Gert.

Book? I looked up. This was the second time in as many days a book had come up.

The Widow Hedwig stared at Gert. "What book?"

Gert shrugged. "The book she reads at night. I see her sometimes when I come downstairs to get a snack.

She hides it away when she hears me coming."

I whispered, and Charming asked, "Where does she hide it?"

"Different places." Gert shrugged again. "Under the frying pan. Beneath the dish towel. Sometimes behind our cloaks hanging by the door—although not mine, not now." She flicked a glance at her mother before continuing. "And once in the flour bin. She sneezed three days straight after that."

"The flour bin." Charming frowned. "But not in her own bedchamber? No one would find it there, surely."

"Bedchamber?" The widow pulled back her chin and stared at the prince. "Whyever would she have a bedchamber?"

Gert nodded. "She's only a step—"

"Scullery maid," said the widow. Firmly. "She's our scullery maid, and we provide her a lovely spot, here on the hearth, where she curls up each night, warm and cozy by the fire."

"On the stones?" Ulff stared at the fireplace, cold and fireless now. "That doesn't sound cozy."

I wrote "Sleeps on stones" in my notes. It made me sorely grateful for my large soft bed at the castle. But in truth, a stone fireplace was a cloud of feathers next

to the spot I not long ago slept in at Swill Cottage—
huddled on the floor under my brothers' bed, a dung-
crusted boot for a pillow, a frigid winter wind howling
through the gaps in the wall.

clues

- Belongings (all missing):
  —only the clothes she wears
  each day
  —plus a book she hides when
  she hears someone coming
- No bedchamber
- Sleeps on stones

Charming had begun overturning pans and dishcloths, cloaks and baskets, searching the kitchen for the scullery maid's book. I tucked away my notes, and Ulff and I hunted through the pantry. We looked on shelves, behind bottles, in bags of rice.

But turned up no book.

14

A Maiden of a Maid

Charming crossed his arms over his breastplate. "Cinderella is gone, and so is the only thing she owns." He held his chin in his armored hand. "But why? And where did they go?"

"Ask about her friends," I whispered.

"Quite right." He turned to the Widow Hedwig.

I held my pencil ready.

"Do her friends have books?" he asked.

The widow frowned in confusion.

I sighed.

Ulff shook his head.

Marge said nothing. She was busy

dawdling about the kitchen, poking her bill into baskets and bins.

I whispered again.

"Ah! That makes much more sense." Charming turned back to the widow. "Who *are* her friends?"

"Friends?" The widow stared at him. "She has no friends. She's a scullery maid. She hasn't time for friends."

I scribbled "No friends." Then wanted to rub it out. They seemed the saddest words I could write about a person. Most likely because until I met Ulff, and then the prince, I could have written those very words about myself.

"And even if she did," Elfrida was saying, "who'd be friends with her?"

Gert snorted. "I can't believe *she's* the one who got a fairy godmother."

I looked up. "Fairy godmother?"

"Pffft." The Widow Hedwig waved the idea away. "The silly ramblings of an addlebrained maid. She's always been jealous of my lovely, elegant daughters."

Ulff frowned. "Truly?"

He looked at Elfrida, hiking her skirt up in a most

unlovely way, and Gert, digging an inelegant bit of breakfast from her teeth.

The widow raised her chin. "*Truly.* That girl is always making up stories to make herself seem better than she is—noble ancestors, loving parents, riches in waiting."

I whispered. Charming nodded.

"And *has* she?" he asked. "Noble ancestors? Loving parents? Riches waiting for her somewhere?"

"Of course not," said the widow, her voice gone high and warbly. "She's no proof who her parents were, nor claim to riches whatsoever. She's simply bitter, just as she was about staying home from the ball. So she dreamed up some foolish thing about a fairy godmother promising her a ball gown."

"And a carriage," said Elfrida.

"And some sort of letter," said Gert, "to prove she's truly—"

The Widow Hedwig clapped a hand over Gert's mouth. "Our scullery maid," she said.

I started to write that down, too. Then stopped. Prove she's truly a scullery maid? Whyever would she want to prove *that*? Most anyone would want to prove the opposite.

But Charming had latched onto something else the widow had said.

"Ball gown." He narrowed his eyes. "Would that happen to be a *blue* ball gown?"

"Of course not," the widow said again. "There's no gown. There's no such thing as a fairy godmother."

"Well, yes." Charming sighed. "That *is* a bit of a sticky wicket."

He frowned, pondering this. I ran a finger down my notes, trying to puzzle out what they meant. Ulff pushed a hand under his lumpy cap to give his head a good scratch and his thoughts a good think.

In all the pondering and puzzling and thinking, we'd all of us quite forgotten about Marge.

Until—

Clack. Clack-clack. Clack.

We looked up. Or rather, down.

The goose had stopped dawdling about the kitchen and was now pecking at the doorway to the pantry.

Clack. Clack.

"Marge!" Charming reached to catch her head. "Stop that. It's rude to peck people's woodwork."

Marge stopped. But when she turned, she held in her bill a bit of shimmery blue fabric. It had been snagged on a splinter of wood, and she'd unsnagged it.

Charming leaned down to tug it free. Marge dug in her webbed feet and tugged back. Charming wrenched. Marge wrenched harder. Finally, Charming blew out a sigh, wedged open her bill with one armored finger, and pulled the fabric loose. Marge hissed and gabbled away.

Charming held the scrap in the palm of his gauntlet. "Why that looks like it's from—"

"A blue ball gown." Ulff nodded. Then frowned. He poked his boot against something on the pantry floor. "And is that—?"

He crouched down and pulled something from a crack between the planks. He held it up. It was an odd-looking bean, bulging and slightly blue.

Charming took it from him and lifted it to the light.

"Exactly like the beans the maiden brought to the ball!" he said.

"She brought beans to a ball?" Elfrida frowned.

"And then cleaned the library." Gert let out a snort. "She doesn't sound much fun."

Elfrida shook her head. "*I* sure wouldn't turn the village upside down trying to find her."

But the prince was too busy sorting through clues to take mind of them.

"At the ball, the maiden had with her a handful of beans," he said. "She must have dropped one here." He studied the spot on the pantry floor where Ulff had plucked the bean from the plank. "Perhaps when she caught her dress." He rubbed the splinter on the doorway where the scrap had snagged. "Perhaps as she was trying to pull it free."

He tapped an armored finger to his lips as he turned full circle, surveying the room.

He frowned. "But what business would that lovely young maiden have in the widow's pantry?"

"She might have business," I pointed out, "if she lives here."

Charming stared at me. "That's it! She *lives* here."

He turned to the Widow Hedwig and her daughters. And frowned.

"But none of you fit the shoe," he said. He shook his head. "And the only other person who lives here"—his eyes grew wide—"is the step-scullery maid!"

He turned to me.

"Nobbin," he said. "The step-scullery maid is the mysterious maiden. We know who has my handkerchief."

I nodded. I even wrote in my notes, "Maid = Maiden."

But we still didn't know where she—or the hanky—had gone.

15

A Trail of Beans

"Cinderella is the scullery maid. The scullery maid is the mysterious maiden in blue. So it's Cinderella that has my hanky." Charming blew out a breath. "And my luck along with it."

He clanked down the widow's front walk, staring ahead at the stone pathway and sorting these new thoughts. Marge waddled at his side. Ulff and I followed. Ulff carried the shoe, holding it as far to his side as his arm would reach. I'd rustled my notes and pencil back into my tunic. The scrap of gown and the blue bean now rattled among the coins in my pouch.

"And the book as well," said Ulff. "Or is it two books?" He scratched his head. "It's all so twisty."

I scuffed over the stone walk, tumbling this thought in my head. It *was* twisty. But the more I thought about it, the more I was sure I'd untwisted it.

"It's just the one," I said. "One maiden. One book. It was Cinderella's only possession. She kept it hidden from the widow."

"To stop her snatching it away, most like," said Ulff.

I nodded. And tried to untwist the next bit.

"Gert said she sometimes hid it behind the cloaks," I said. "What if, one time, Cinderella heard Gert coming and quick slipped it into the *pocket* of a cloak?"

Ulff stared at me. "Then didn't have a chance to get it out again before Gert put the cloak on and wore it out of the house."

I nodded again. "To the king's garden party."

"Where she left it behind!" Ulff blinked. "And it landed in the lost and found. Then at the ball, when the maiden shook it—"

"—the book tumbled from the pocket," I said.

I'd thought Charming was paying little attention. But now, he stopped and turned back to look at us.

"Is *that* why she was eager to see the lost and found?" he said. "To find her book?"

He let out a long breath. His face crumpled. His

head drooped. He stared at his armored feet and shook his head.

"I thought she harbored a true zest for folding and sorting," he said.

I cast a look at Ulff. He cast a wide-eyed look back.

"Well," I said. "She probably did have a zest. I imagine."

"Right," said Ulff. "Her being a step-scullery maid and all."

"She did want the book, it's true," I said, "but—she—uh, used her folding and sorting talent to find it."

Ulff nodded. "It was a combination, most like."

We'd reached the end of the walk—and Darnell, dozing beside the lamppost. Charming unlatched the gate. A heavy sigh shook his slumping shoulders.

"Besides," I said, "she did find the cloak for us. The one you promised to send back to Gert."

"Yes." The prince straightened. "There is that."

He looked up.

And jerked back his head.

"Sweet persimmon!" he said. "I always thought this the quiet side of the village."

His gaze skimmed the lane that ran in front of the widow's house. Several villagers lurked there. When they spied us, they quick made as if they had business thereabouts.

The tailor turned to rub his sleeve over an invisible spot on his shop window.

Three dwarfs developed a sudden interest in a barrel outside the cooper's shop, running their palms over it and nodding, as if the barrel were a fascinating new invention. I had a suspicion the other four dwarfs might well be hiding inside it.

The miller's daughter darted through a nearby gate. She must've noticed straightaway she'd ducked into the village pigsty, for she darted out again and lurched down the lane, shaking pig muck from her feet.

I thought I spotted the man new to the village, the one in the hooded cloak I'd seen earlier in the square. But he fast hobbled around a corner before I could be sure.

Ulff ran his gaze up and down the lane and shook his head.

"Twigg folk do get nosy," he said.

I nodded. The villagers might have been cranky and worn out after a morning trying on the shoe, but they would all of them tumble over each other to see if the prince found a fit at the widow's house.

A familiar jangle interrupted my thought. Ulff and I turned to glimpse Stiltskin swerve his cart into an alleyway.

"And that one's nosier than most," said Ulff.

It was true. Every corner we'd turned lately, we seemed to run into Mr. Stiltskin.

But as I watched the peddler, I spied something else. The cart's wheel had kicked up something from the cobblestones. It was a small something, and at first I paid scant attention, thinking it a pebble.

But as it fell to the cobblestones, a slant of afternoon sun struck that small something.

It glimmered faintly blue.

I frowned. A blue pebble? Surely not.

I scrabbled up the lane to retrieve the small something before I lost the spot where it had landed. I plucked it from the cobbles and turned it in my palm. It was odd-shaped and bulging. And yes, tinged with blue.

I scrabbled back to the prince and Ulff.

"Another bean." I held it out.

Charming, Ulff, and Darnell peered down at it.

Marge pushed her bill in for a look. She let out a honk, flipped the bean from my palm, and stalked off. In disgust, it seemed. If a goose could be disgusted.

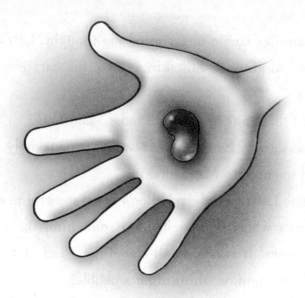

I bent to retrieve it.

And wondered at this. Marge didn't like beans. That much had been plain when the maiden—Cinderella—offered her a handful of them at the ball.

But this seemed more than dislike. It seemed like outrage, as if she held a grudge against the beans.

But did she begrudge *all* beans? I studied the bean in my palm. Or just *these* beans, the bulgy blue ones?

Charming took the bean from me and held it up to the sunlight. He squinted at it.

"Exactly like the one in the pantry." He glanced about. "They seem to be everywhere."

"Leastways everywhere Cinderella's been," said Ulff.

Charming nodded. Then stared at him. "I believe you have the right of it, Ulff! She clearly dropped this bean, just as she dropped the bean in the pantry. She must be dropping them wherever she goes. We need simply follow the trail of beans to find her."

He set off up the lane. Darnell, Ulff, and I clopped and tromped behind. Marge gabbled and complained, but eventually waddled to catch up.

We scanned the cobblestones, the prince holding the bean before him, as if it would lead him to the next.

And it did.

We reached the alleyway Stiltskin had jangled into. It was cobbled and dark, the afternoon sunlight venturing only a few paces into the narrow passage between the shops. There was no sign of the peddler there now.

But the prince spotted something else.

"Ho!" he cried.

He clanked up the alley. Wedged against the bricks of the tailor shop and nearly hidden beneath a wheelbarrow was a small bulge of blue.

The prince plucked it up.

"You see?" He turned to Ulff and me. "We're truly on the trail now."

He set off again up the dark alley, holding both beans before him this time.

When he reached the end of the alley, he turned and clanked up the next lane.

And back down again.

And around the corner.

And up the next lane.

And the next.

And the lane after that.

Ulff, Darnell, Marge, and I followed at his heels.

We scoured every street and alley in Twigg, every gutter and doorway, around each corner and behind every shop, until Marge's short goose legs nearly gave out and we had to prop her onto Darnell's saddle.

We covered the whole of the village.

And found no more beans.

At last we reached the edge of Twigg. Charming stopped and pushed back his drooping plume. The sun was slanting down the other side of the sky. Ulff's belly let out a woeful growl. I clapped a hand to my own belly to stop it growling in sympathy. We'd not eaten since we'd picked the last crumbs of gingerbread from Cook's kitchen towel early that morning.

The prince studied the odd blue bulges in his hand.

"Two beans," he said, "make a very short trail."

16

A Rider in Black

Early the next morning—it seemed all early mornings with Charming of late—we set off for jousting training. It would be his last practice before the tournament began that very afternoon.

We crunched across the gray morning courtyard: Charming, Ulff, Marge, and me. Angelica was not with us this time. We'd sneaked a roundabout way out of the castle to keep from passing her bedchamber.

"I'm not eager to tell her why I've not brought the hanky with me," the prince explained.

The arena builders were already at work, their bang and clatter hammering over the castle grounds—

and through my sleep-fogged head. I squinted into the morning sun and saw the tall poles towering over the tournament grounds.

As we approached the stables, Charming stopped dead. Ulff and I, scuffling along behind, nearly plowed into him.

We stumbled back.

But the prince paid us little notice.

He stood staring, his mouth pressed in a grim line. Ulff and I followed his gaze.

A rider, clad head to toe in black armor and sitting astride a massive black steed, rode away from the stables through the morning mist. Horse and rider cantered across the meadow, leapt the fence at the other end, and disappeared into the shadows of the trees.

"Sorry to keep you waiting, your highness."

I blinked and turned toward the stables. Sir Hugo, red-faced and out of breath, hurried out, leading Darnell.

Charming still stared at the spot where the rider had disappeared. He narrowed his eyes. "Was that—?"

Sir Hugo darted a quick glance in the direction of the rider.

"A—ah—another competitor, yes." He swallowed.

"He needed a few . . . details. About the tournament. Where it's to be held. When it will start. Which is soon, very soon." He patted Darnell, who blew a snort in his face. "So we'd better get to practicing."

Charming stared for some moments more before tearing his gaze away to give Darnell a rub on the muzzle.

With Sir Hugo pushing, Ulff pulling, and me fixed to catch him when he slid off, we got the prince mounted and facing the right direction.

Marge stood in the gravel, waiting for him to lift her to the saddle.

He shook his head at her. "Not this time, I fear, dear goose. I must set my full attention to the tilt."

I crouched and wrapped my arms around her, thinking to carry her to a pile of straw. I gave a heave—

—but barely lifted her flappy goose feet from the gravel. Barking bloomers! The prince did not jest. This goose was made of pure lead. I heaved again. And again. Then gave up heaving and simply shooed her to the straw. She gave a grumbling honk, but shook her tail and settled in.

Sir Hugo trotted to the far end of the tiltyard. Ulff handed the prince his lance.

"You did it before, with the hanky," Ulff told him. "You can do it now without."

Charming nodded and clanked shut his visor. He shook out his arms, rolled his neck, squared his shoulders, and blew out a breath.

"I *can* do this," he said, more to himself than to anyone else.

As he rode Darnell onto the tiltyard, I felt a prickle on the back of my neck. I turned to see what looked to be the flutter of a dark cloak disappearing around the corner of the stable.

But when I blinked, the flutter was gone. I shook my head. It must've been a bit of tall grass stirring in the shadows. I turned back to the tiltyard.

Sir Hugo gave the signal. Charming dug in his heels, and Darnell thundered down the list.

Whiff.

The prince's lance swung wide.

And then kept swinging around till it swung Charming right off the saddle.

Clunk.

"*Ooof!*"

He landed on his backplate in a pile of straw.

He rocked back and forth for a moment before rolling

to his side and climbing to his feet. Darnell ambled back and touched the prince with his muzzle.

Charming righted his helmet, caught his breath, led his steed back to the start of the tiltyard, and seated himself in his saddle once more.

Sir Hugo gave the signal. Charming dug in. Darnell thundered.

Whiff.

Clunk.

"*Ooof!*"

The prince rocked on his back a bit longer this time before climbing to his feet and leading Darnell back.

Whiff.

Clunk.

"*Ooof!*"

Whiff.

Clunk.

"*Ooof!*"

After the fourth time, Charming rocked. And rocked. Until Ulff darted an alarmed look at me, I darted a panicked look back, and we scrabbled down to the tiltyard to the prince.

As we knelt by his side, he raised his visor.

"Ho . . . chaps." He gasped out a wheezing breath.

"That last fall seems to have . . . knocked the very wind . . . from my lungs."

He lay there, blinking and gulping for a long moment. At last he raised his hands in the air. We each of us took hold of one and wrenched him up. He swayed, but stayed on his feet. Ulff and I positioned ourselves on either side in case he buckled.

"Yes. Well." He gathered up Darnell's reins. "I believe that's enough training."

As Sir Hugo gathered up his signal flag and Charming's lance, the prince led Darnell to the stables. Ulff and I scrambled behind.

But as the prince reached the stable door, he stopped and turned back toward the spot where the black-armored rider had earlier disappeared into the trees. Darnell nickered and nuzzled the prince's cheek. Marge lay her head and neck against Charming's leg.

Ulff patted the prince's shoulder plate.

"You can't let that fellow sink your confidence," he told him. "Sure, he's tall and shiny and fearsome-mean in all that black armor. And sure, his horse is enormous, with muscles bulging in places I never knew a horse *had* muscles—beg pardon, Darnell." He gave the steadfast steed a pat. "And sure, the two of them together look like they could unsaddle an opponent before anyone even saw the flick of the lance, but . . . um . . . where was I going with this?" He wrinkled his brow and gave his head a scratch. "Oh, yeah! Looks aren't everything. You have to trust what's inside." He tapped a finger to the prince's breastplate.

Charming shook his head. "That's entirely the problem," he said. "What's inside. I recognize that armor—and that steed. The rider was my father. And Sir Hugo is helping him train."

17

A Prince Unarmored

Father?" Ulff's voice was a strangled yelp.

Charming had turned to lead Darnell into the stables. Marge waddled along at their heels.

Ulff and I stood planted outside the stable door, not moving, nor even blinking, as if we'd grown roots in that very spot.

At last Ulff shook his head, clearing his muddled thoughts, and trotted after them.

I shook off my muddle, too, and followed.

Our scuffling footsteps on the stone floor echoed through the cool darkness of the stable.

We caught up to the

prince outside Darnell's stall.

Ulff pushed his way in front of him, between the prince and the stall. He looked directly in the prince's face.

"*Your* father?" he said. "The king?"

Charming reached around Ulff to unlatch the stall gate. He swung it open, swirling the aroma of warm horse and fresh hay over us. I pulled in a deep breath of it. Little wonder the prince spent so much time here. The quiet and the calm and the sweet stable scent seemed to steady me a small measure.

The prince led Darnell into the stall. "You saw his portrait in the library." He uncinched Darnell's saddle. "All in black, astride his fierce black steed—as he was when he won the tournament. It's the same armor. There can be no mistake."

Ulff frowned. "But not the same steed. Surely. That horse must be"—he glanced at Darnell and lowered his voice to a whisper—"gone some twenty years or more. At least."

"But one so much like him as to be his offspring," said the prince. "Or his offspring's offspring."

He lifted the saddle from Darnell's back and heaved it onto the wooden saddle rack on the wall. He turned back, letting out a breath from the effort of it.

140

"My father clearly has no trust in me," he said. "And why would he? I've given him no reason." He ran a brush down Darnell's flank. "He's entering the tournament to ensure that *someone* defends the family honor. He's jousting to keep the cup at the castle."

Ulff raised his eyebrows. "He wouldn't."

I shook my head. "He couldn't."

"Your father said—"

"And he truly meant—"

"When he gave you the hanky—"

"The hanky," said Charming, "that I lost."

He gave Darnell a final brush and filled his feed bucket with oats. He backed from the stall and latched the gate, then pulled off his gauntlets and set them on the floor next to his helmet.

He turned his back toward me.

"Can you unfasten the buckles, Nobbin?" he said. "Once I get the breastplate off, I can do the rest myself."

I stared at him, openmouthed.

Ulff gulped. "The . . . rest?" he said.

Charming took a long look down at his armor. "I can't think what need I have for it now."

18

A Shambles in the Library

N o armor!" said Ulff.

He gave a sharp glance about the courtyard. It was early still, but castle servants were about. Gardeners weeded and watered. A kitchen maid stepped outside to dump a pail of slop. One of the pages scurried past toward the guard garrison.

Ulff lowered his voice.

"I've never seen the prince with no armor," he said. "It was like seeing him in his"—he cupped a hand over his mouth and leaned toward me—*"underthings."*

"He was wearing a doublet," I said. "And hosen. He was fully clothed." I gave a thought to this. "But you're right—it felt unseemly looking at him like that."

"Worse than unseemly," said Ulff. "Worrisome. What if he doesn't—?"

He stopped.

I stopped, too. And swallowed.

"—put it back on?" I said.

We stared at each other, eyes wide.

Charming had taken Marge to the moat. He'd said it was so she could have a long swim. I thought it was more so the prince could have a long think.

Ulff and I had taken the chance to scarper off to the library. We told the prince it was to place the glass slipper in the lost and found where it rightly belonged and, while we were there, retrieve Gert's cloak.

But we had a truer mission: Find evidence that the king could *not* have been the rider in black—evidence that would convince Charming to put his armor back on. Quick. For the tournament was only a few hours away.

We turned toward the castle—

—and near ran smack into Sir Roderick. He'd been striding along, head bent in thought, from the opposite direction.

"Oh!" I took a step back.

"Oooh!" Ulff grabbed my arm to stop himself stumbling.

"Ah!" Roderick jerked back his head.

And for a sliver of a second, he looked as taken by surprise as we were, as if Ulff and I had sprung into his path, fully formed from thin air.

But only for that sliver, then villainy oozed back over his face.

"You two." He ran his usual black scowl up and down the whole of us. "A lowly guard and . . . whatever it is *you* are." He flicked a hand toward me. "You should learn to watch your step."

He glared at us till we stepped aside, then stalked past, his robes whipping our faces.

Ulff turned to watch him go. I gave a glance the other way, wondering where he'd been. From the direction he'd come were only storehouses and the rear tower.

Ulff shook his head. "Between him and that Stiltskin fellow," he muttered, "it's a wonder this kingdom has *any* peace."

We waited to make sure he was well and truly gone, then tucked through the kitchen garden and slipped into the castle by a side door.

As we crept past the kitchen, a gust of gingery sweetness billowed out. Ulff's belly gave a rumbling moan. He stuck his nose in the air, his nostrils quavering like a dog sniffing out a bone. But he did not slow his step. Nor even falter. I was sorely impressed. Our quest was direr to him even than gingerbread.

We turned at the end of the passage, scuttered down the hallway to the library, and stopped before the great oak door.

I pulled the bolt. It unlatched with a soft click. We eased the door open, slipped inside, and stood for a moment to let our eyes adjust to the dimness.

"Oh." Ulff's voice was a hushed groan.

I followed his gaze.

"Oh." I let out my own hushed groan.

For the lost and found—neatly folded and sorted only a day before—was now a towering swirl of sleeves, straps, and strings. Scarves and stockings hung over the edges of tables. Shoes, gloves, and pouches were tossed about the floor.

I stared at it. "Who could've done this?"

I thought back to our run-in with Sir Roderick. Could he have been coming from the library? I frowned. It seemed doubtful. He would have had to circle near

146

the entire castle to get back to the courtyard from the direction he'd come.

"I don't know." Ulff planted his fists on his hips. "But I can guess who'll have to clean it up."

I nodded. And sighed. The pile was a mess already. We wouldn't do it much more harm to rustle through for Gert's cloak.

I dug through the pile on one table. Ulff set the glass slipper on a high shelf to save it being broken and dug through the pile on the next. And through the things scattered about the floor. And behind chairs. And on shelves. And under the rug.

Until finally, Ulff collapsed onto a bench.

"It's not here." His words came out in a breath.

I sat back on my heels. "I think other things are missing, too."

I closed my eyes, trying to picture the lost and found from the night of the ball.

"There was a boy's boot," I said. "And a lady's buckled shoe."

Ulff tipped his head to study the piles. "And a man's leather belt," he said. "I took notice because I thought I might get the village girdler to fashion one like it."

I climbed to my feet. We'd failed the prince in our

first task, the easy one: Retrieve Gert's cloak. I crossed my fingers—hard—that we would not fail him in the second.

We made our way to the other end of the library, to the gleaming gold tournament cup. Behind it, at the end of the long line of tournament portraits, hung the painting of Charming's father.

We studied it for a long while, saying nothing.

At last, Ulff blew out a breath.

"The prince was right," he said. "It had to be the king at the tiltyard. Riding a look-alike steed."

I nodded. "There's no mistaking that armor. Or his majesty."

I pointed to the king's armored hand, clasped to his chest. A corner of an embroidered lace handkerchief, exactly like the hanky the king gave Charming, peeked out from the gleaming black gauntlet.

19

A List of Clues

The king," said Ulff. "Our very king."

He paced before the tournament cup, his footsteps creaking over the wide planks of the library floor.

"Charming's own *father*." I paced, too, in the opposite direction.

Ulff reached the library wall and turned to pace the other way. "The prince would never wield a lance against him."

I nodded. "He'd sooner bow out in dishonor."

"And we'd never get him back in his armor again," said Ulff.

I slowed my pace and tried to think of this— Charming with no honor. And no armor. I couldn't form a picture of it. Honor and armor were the core of the prince. Take them away, and you may as well wrench out his heart.

"We have to stop the king riding in the tournament," I said.

"Stop him?" Ulff came to a dead halt. His voice rose to a screech. "He's the *king*. Our very king."

"I know," I said. "Charming's fa—"

Now *I* came to a dead halt.

"He's Charming's father," I said.

Ulff looked at me, eyes narrowed. "Yesss," he said. Slowly to make sure I understood. "That's why our prince is a prince."

"And," I said, "it's why the king gave Charming the hanky. He *wants* the prince to win the tournament—if he can."

Ulff bristled. "If he can? Of course he can. Well, if he *thinks* he can. If he has the confidence for it. Or has the hanky what gives him the confidence." He shook his head. "If the prince hadn't lost the hanky, the king would have no—"

He looked up.

I nodded.

"We have to find that maiden," he said. "Quick."

I pulled out my paper and pencil so we could list everything we knew about the mysterious maiden, Cinderella.

"Well." Ulff rubbed a hand over the bristles of his chin. "She's the Widow Hedwig's step-scullery maid."

I nodded and wrote it down.

"But," I said, "she's trying *not* to be the widow's step-scullery maid."

Ulff raised an eyebrow. "I don't blame her there. But she's also jealous of Gert and Elfrida." He shook his head. "And that's a shame, since she has no other friends."

I started to write this. Then stopped.

"But is she really?" I tapped my pencil against my lip. "Jealous? And friendless? We only have the widow's word for either of those."

"True." Ulff scrunched his face in thought. "But you should write it down. It's a clue either way."

I nodded and scribbled it down.

"She has a ball gown," I said. "And a lace wrap and a pair of glass slippers."

"Nope." Ulff shook his head. "She only has the one. We have the other."

"Good point."

I scratched out "a pair of."

"She loves books," I said.

"And beans. The blue, bulgy kind." Ulff wrinkled his nose. "Can't say I've ever seen that particular variety before, but they don't look tasty."

"Marge doesn't think so, either," I said. "What else?"

Ulff stared at the ceiling. "She can sort and fold like nobody I've ever seen. Even if she was only ever doing it to get her book back. And"—he held a finger in the air—"she's afraid of clocks."

I pressed my pencil to the page. Then looked up. "Was she really afraid, though?"

Ulff shrugged. "She ran out of there in a hurry as soon as the big one in the ballroom started bonging."

"But maybe she just needed to get back to the widow's house to put the mutton in the oven."

Ulff raised his eyebrows. "She was afraid of the widow finding her out. That would sure scare me."

I couldn't disagree.

I stopped writing. I was near the end of the page. It surprised me how much we knew about Cinderella. She was:

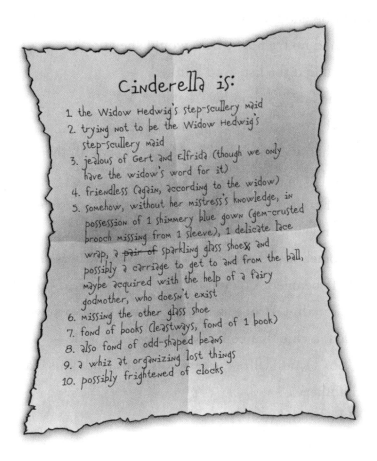

Cinderella is:

1. the Widow Hedwig's step-scullery maid
2. trying not to be the Widow Hedwig's step-scullery maid
3. jealous of Gert and Elfrida (though we only have the widow's word for it)
4. friendless (again, according to the widow)
5. somehow, without her mistress's knowledge, in possession of 1 shimmery blue gown (gem-crusted brooch missing from 1 sleeve), 1 delicate lace wrap, a ~~pair of~~ sparkling glass shoes and possibly a carriage to get to and from the ball, maybe acquired with the help of a fairy godmother, who doesn't exist
6. missing the other glass shoe
7. fond of books (leastways, fond of 1 book)
8. also fond of odd-shaped beans
9. a whiz at organizing lost things
10. possibly frightened of clocks

I stared at the list. Then wrote one more thing:

10. possibly frightened of clocks

11 missing

I thought about this. Being any kind of maid for the Widow Hedwig—and her demanding daughters—

155

would be enough to make anyone run away. But if she truly had no friends, where would she go?

I studied the list. And blinked.

"The fairy godmother," I said.

Ulff frowned. "The one she made up?"

"What if she didn't?" I said. "What if the fairy godmother is real?"

Ulff considered this. "I suppose she had to get the dress and shoes from *somebody*."

"Somebody," I said, "who might know where she is."

Ulff beamed a triumphant smile. I beamed a smile back. Finally! At long last, we had a real lead, somewhere to start, a clue that could break this case wide—

"So," said Ulff, "where do we find this fairy godmother?"

I blinked. "Well . . ."

I studied the list again. I ran my finger over everything Cinderella said she got from this possible fairy godmother, everything she needed for the ball. The gown. The wrap. The carriage. The—

I looked up. "The shoe. Of all the things this godmother gave Cinderella, it's the only one she left behind. If this fairy godmother gave it to her—"

"—wouldn't the godmother expect her to bring it back?" said Ulff.

I nodded. And tried to think who had seemed most interested in the shoe when Charming took it to the village. Everyone, actually. But that's when they all thought Charming wanted to marry the missing maiden. They none of them cared a fig about the shoe. They just wanted to live in the castle.

But now, with no marriage involved, anyone who showed interest in the shoe would have their own reason.

"You think the shoe can lead us to the fairy godmother?" said Ulff.

"I think"—I studied the glass shoe sitting on the library shelf—"the shoe may lead the fairy godmother to us."

20

A Huddle of Merchants

Ulff and I—and the shoe—set off once more for the village. We crept across the drawbridge, not wanting Charming to spy us from the moat. The hammer and bang of the workmen well covered our footsteps. I chanced a glimpse over my shoulder. The tops of the king's pennants already fluttered over the near-finished arena.

I picked up my stride. By the time we returned, the arena *would* be finished and the tournament nigh to begin.

Ulff and I made our way down the roadway at a trot. When we reached Twigg, we turned up the high street and headed straight for the shoemaker's shop.

We stood for a moment outside the door. Ulff blew out a breath. I squared my shoulders, then pulled the latch and swung open the door.

At the jingle of the bell and burst of breeze that whisked us into the shop, the shopkeepers started. They jerked their heads toward the door.

I jerked my head, too. For there were four of them: the shoemaker and his wife, yes, but also the dressmaker from next door and the lacemaker from down the lane.

They were huddled around the counter at the back of the shop, and we'd plainly interrupted them in something.

Something they plainly wanted to hide.

The shoemaker's wife bustled her round body to straighten a shoe display, as if that was what she'd meant to do all along, and knocked a sturdy pair of shears to the floor. The lacemaker quick straightened to her full bony height, bumping her head against a ceiling beam. The small, hunched dressmaker held her mouth open wide, as if we'd stopped her in the midst of a sentence and she was too surprised to close it. The shoemaker reached for the dropped shears and banged one of his knobby knees on the counter stool.

I stared at them.

A round woman.

A tall woman.

A hunched woman.

And a knobby-kneed man.

"You were at the ball!" I blurted before I could stop myself—before I even knew there was a blurt to stop.

The four of them slid glances at each other. For a moment, none of them spoke.

Then the shoemaker swallowed.

"We were." He raised his chin. "As was everyone in the village."

"But you"—I narrowed my eyes—"you were the ones trying to get close to the mysterious maiden."

Ulff leaned in and peered at the shoemaker. His eyes popped wide.

"That's right!" He pointed. "I danced with you."

"I, uh"—the shoemaker swallowed again—"I'm sure you're mistaken."

Ulff narrowed his eyes. "I'm sure I'm not."

"You wanted to hear about her garments," I said. "Her gown, her wrap"—I gestured toward the glass slipper in Ulff's hand—"her shoe."

Ulff looked at the shoe. Then the shopkeepers. His mouth dropped open.

"You're her fairy godmothers!" he said.

The four of them stared at him, then at each other, their faces knotted in confusion.

"Her what?"

"Fairy who?"

"I assure you—"

"—we're no such thing!"

I studied them. *Could* they be the fairy godmothers? In one way, it made sense. Their shops weren't as bustling as they once were. If they had dressed a lovely girl in their finest creations and sent her off to the ball, the entire village would be awestruck at her finery. And scrabbling to buy such finery for themselves.

But—I thought back to the ball—these four shopkeepers had seemed the *most* awestruck by Cinderella. And if this was their plan, to dress her up and send her out, they never did the most important part—tell all those villagers that *they* were the ones who created the finery.

Plus, they were now staring at us in such flabbergasted astonishment that, even though Ulff wasn't entirely convinced, I couldn't help but believe them.

"No," I said slowly, "I don't think you are. But you were interested in her for *some* reason."

The shoemaker looked at the other three.

The dressmaker gulped.

The lacemaker fluttered a hand at her throat.

His wife let out a sigh.

"You may as well tell them," she said.

The shoemaker turned to us.

"Yes," he said. "We wanted to get close to her. We were trying to, well"—he flicked a glance at his wife—"eavesdrop, if you must know. We wanted to find out where she'd gotten such fine garments. The trade in our own shops has slowed to a near halt. We simply wanted to know who'd been stealing our business."

He fell silent. And stared at the floor.

"We may be able to help you on that score," I said.

He looked up.

"Would you be willing to place the glass shoe in your shop window?" I said. "It may attract attention."

The shoemaker's eyebrows shot up. "I daresay it would."

"It may attract the one who gave it to the maiden," said Ulff.

21

A Shoe in the Window

The shoemaker placed the shoe in his shop window, on a stand draped in plush velvet.

The dressmaker and lacemaker grumbled but returned to their shops.

The shoemaker, not wanting to hide away in his backroom workshop, brought some leather out to the shop counter to cut.

His wife took up her feather duster once more, flicking it over the window and the velvet-draped stand and the shoe itself, until every last dust speck had either been whisked away or given up and gone into hiding. All the while, she kept a sharp eye on the window and on anyone who happened by.

Ulff and I tucked ourselves behind the drapery at the edge of the window. From there we could observe anyone who looked interested in the shoe without those anyones observing us back.

We didn't wait long to start our observing.

The Woodcutters trooped up the lane, all four of them: Mr. and Mrs. Woodcutter and their children, Hansel and Gretel. It seemed they would simply troop on past, until Hansel flicked a gaze at the shop window, stopped, looked again, then tugged on his father's arm and pointed.

I slid a look at Ulff and raised my eyebrows. Could the woodcutter be Cinderella's fairy godmother? He was a near artist with a log of wood and an ax. Could he also have the skill to carve a shoe of glass?

But when I looked back, Hansel was pointing to the slipper, then at his father's foot. He and Gretel and even Mrs. Woodcutter laughed. The woodcutter gave them an embarrassed smile and ruffled Hansel's hair, then the four of them trooped off down the lane.

I shook my head at Ulff. The Woodcutters were none of them the fairy godmother. They'd only stopped to make a jest about the woodcutter getting his toe stuck in the shoe.

In but a few minutes, the miller's daughter stopped for a look. Then the lovely young woman who lived with the dwarfs in their cottage in the woods. They were both of them known about the village for their sharp way of dressing. Well, as sharp as Twigg life allowed. But they both simply gave the shoe a longing look, sighed, and went on their way.

The woman from the boot-shaped cottage tried to take a peek, but had to run after three of her children to stop them climbing the butcher's lamppost.

The old man in the hooded cloak hovered at the edge of the window for a bit. He sneaked a look at the shoe, then over his shoulder, then hobbled away. I peered at him through the gap between drapery and window. Little wonder he hobbled. He looked to be wearing mismatched boots.

A weary mule clopped by, pulling a jangly cart. Rumpelstiltskin sat in the driver's seat, darting his quick glance here and there at the shops in the lane. When his glance fell on the shoe shop, his mouth fell open. He pulled hard on the reins to halt the mule.

He glanced about again, looking to see that no one was watching. Then he climbed from the cart, all elbows and knees, and ambled into the shop.

The shoemaker's wife was still feather dusting the window. When the bell over the door jingled, she jumped. The shoemaker looked up from his leather work. Ulff and I froze, two soldiers standing at attention behind a drapery.

Mrs. Shoemaker tucked the duster into her skirts and turned to the peddler.

"May we help you?" she said.

Stiltskin raised his hat to her, but his gleaming eyes never left the shoe in the window.

"I've come to make a trade," he said, still gazing at the shoe. "I've a near-new pair of work boots in my cart, hardly mud-crusted at all. I'll swap them to you for that poor lonely slipper in the window. Two shoes for one. It's a bad trade on my part. You should take it before I come to my senses and change my mind."

The shoemaker cleared his throat. He cut a look to the drapes, where Ulff and I hid.

Stiltskin cut a look, too. I scarce breathed.

"That shoe is not for sale nor trade, I'm afraid," said the shoemaker.

Stiltskin cut his look away from the drapery.

"My good shoemaker," he said. "Everything is for sale or trade."

He pulled open his great coat. It clanked and rattled from the pots and spoons and pipes and jewels stashed in it.

He reached inside. "Perhaps this fine flute," he said.

"I don't think so," said the shoemaker.

"A fragrant cologne?" said Stiltskin.

The shoemaker shook his head.

"Perhaps you would change your mind if I offered you—" He reached into his pocket for another item of trade.

I leaned one way, peering between drapery and window to see what it was.

Ulff leaned the other, peering around the far edge of the drape. He leaned a bit more, and more still, until he leaned too far. His elbow flew out, bumping a shelf and knocking over a spool of thread. The spool tumbled from the shelf and rolled across the rough wood floor, leaving a blue thread unspooling behind it.

Stiltskin waited until the spool rolled to his feet.

He snatched it up in his gnarly-knuckled hand. He studied it for a moment, then strode across the shop and pulled back the drapery.

Ulff gulped.

I blinked.

Stiltskin ran his gaze up and down the both of us, then cast his gaze about the shop.

"No prince this day?" he said.

I kept my lips clamped firmly shut.

But Ulff lifted his chin. "We're perfectly fit to journey out on our own," he said.

"*Are* you?" Stiltskin raised an eyebrow. "And what of His Charmingness? Is he able to prince about on his own?"

Ulff stiffened. "The prince doesn't prince about. He

has duties. Responsibilities. At this very moment, he's taking care of his goo—"

I jabbed an elbow into Ulff's ribs.

"*Goo?*" said Stiltskin. "As in *goose?*" His eyebrows snapped up. "By himself? Alone?"

Ulff clenched his fists. "Of course he's—"

I clamped a hand over his mouth.

"Bfwy mmsf!" Ulff yelped from under my fingers.

"Yes. Well." Stiltskin slid his hand back into his great coat, pocketing whatever small something he had planned to trade for the shoe and the spool of thread as well.

He turned to the shoemaker.

"It's clear you're not interested in a trade," he said. "I shan't bother you longer."

He tipped his hat, gave Ulff and me one more up-and-down look, and loped from the shop. The bell jingled and the door slammed shut behind him.

The shoemaker let out a whoosh of breath.

I leaned closer to the window—and nearly knocked heads with the shoemaker's wife, who'd leaned in, too. Ulff crowded in behind the both of us.

We watched Stiltskin amble to his cart. When he reached it, he whipped a quick glance back at the shop.

Ulff, Mrs. Shoemaker, and I jerked away from the window.

When we dared peer around the frame again, mule, cart, and Stiltskin had trundled off, the cart squeaking and creaking and picking up speed.

I watched it disappear down the lane—

—and caught a flicker of shimmery blue fabric, a tiny corner, fluttering from the peddler's mound of wares at the back.

My eyes popped wide.

I turned to the shoemaker.

"When you traded the gem-crusted brooch, who did you trade it to?"

The shoemaker's Adam's apple bobbed. He glanced at his wife.

"I don't like to admit it," he said, "but I traded it to that fellow." He tipped his head toward the window. "Rumpelstiltskin."

22

A Peddler and His Plan

Rumpelstiltskin? A fairy godmother?" Ulff shuddered. "More like a fairy nightmare."

"But it makes sense." I was pacing again, this time over the shoe shop's creaky floors. "The blue fabric. The brooch. When I saw Cinderella's gown had but one, I thought she'd lost the other. But there was only ever one brooch—the one I fished from the dung and traded to the shoemaker."

The shoemaker darted a glance at his wife, who shot him a glare in return.

"The shoemaker traded it to Skiltskin," I said, "and—"

"Stiltskin put it on the gown!" Ulff's eyes grew wide. Then narrowed. "But that would be doing something nice for someone else." He scratched his head. "That's not like him."

The shoemaker nodded. "That fellow never does a thing but there's something in it for him."

That was true. I turned in my pace and thought back to the times we'd seen Mr. Stiltskin over the past days.

"He wanted an invitation to the ball," I said. "And the king's men wouldn't give him one."

Ulff nodded. "Because he was banned from the castle. For life, if the king has his say."

"So the only way he could get in," I said, "would be to convince someone to bring him as a guest—"

"—and hope the king's men didn't recognize him in his mask," Ulff said. Then frowned. "But he *didn't* get in. He didn't even try. Cinderella came by herself."

I stopped. It was true. I'd watched her slip in myself. But if Stiltskin didn't make a deal with Cinderella to take him—

I looked up. "He sent her in his place."

Ulff frowned. "To what end?"

Mrs. Shoemaker snorted. "What end is there anything with Stiltskin? Pilfering things that don't belong to him."

Ulff nodded. "Last time he was in the castle, he was

caught pilfering from the kitchens. It's what got him banned." He frowned. "But I can't think Cinderella would agree to pilfer *for* him."

"She wouldn't be the first person in the village who got the bad end of one of Stiltskin's bargains." Mrs. Shoemaker turned a sharp look on her husband.

He swallowed. "It's true. He nearly talked me into trading a pair of riding boots not long past."

I frowned. "What was it he tried to trade?"

Mrs. Shoemaker snorted again. "A goose! He wanted a pair of our finest boots in trade for a goose."

23

A Goose in a Pickle

$\mathfrak{A}$ goose?"

I stared at Ulff. Ulff stared back.

"No," he whispered.

We bolted from the shoemaker's shop and down the lane, dodging villagers, including—again—the small old man in the hooded cloak. If Charming had been with us, he would have stopped to ask if that hobbling man were lost, for surely he was.

But Ulff and I had a goose to save, and Stiltskin had a solid start on us.

We left Twigg behind and hurried along the roadway, in and out of folks filing toward the tournament. We passed Swill Cottage and trudged up the hill to the castle. Hunched over and out of breath, we spotted the peddler's cart on the embankment of the moat.

And spotted the peddler. His hands gripped Marge's neck as he tried to wrench her from Charming's grasp.

"Marge!" Ulff called out.

We raced along the embankment.

When we reached them, Charming's face was white. Stiltskin's was twisted in fury.

"The goose is mine," Stiltskin growled. "She ran away from me last time I was at the castle."

"I don't blame her there," said Ulff.

"If she ran away from you," I said, "she doesn't *want* to be yours."

Marge flapped and let out a strangled honk.

"That makes little difference." Stiltskin gave another tug.

Charming cradled Marge to his chest. He reached for her neck, clearly worried for it.

"A goose," said Stiltskin, "has no say."

Ulff glowered. "She has every say!"

I glared. "It's her very—"

But Charming stopped me.

"I fear the peddler has the right of it," he said. "As prince of the kingdom and keeper of the lost and found"—he swallowed—"I'm honor-bound to do what's right. As with the shoes and scarves and left-behind whatnot, it's my duty to return her to"—he swallowed again and choked a bit—"her rightful owner."

Stiltskin gave a nod. "That's more like it," he said.

He let go of his grip on Marge's neck and turned to pull a cage from his cart.

"But"—Charming pulled Marge protectively against his chest—"what proof have you that you are, in fact, her rightful owner?"

Rumpelstiltskin turned back, cage in hand. His mouth twisted into a frightening smile.

"I was hoping you'd ask that," he said.

He slid a hand inside a pocket of his coat and pulled out something soft and white. He held it up.

Charming blinked. "Is that—"

"The tip of a goose feather?" said Stiltskin. "Why, yes. Yes, it is."

He took hold of Marge's wing and stretched it to show the snipped feathers. He placed the tip of the feather from his pocket against a clipped feather on her wing.

"Perfect fit," he said.

And tugged Marge from Charming's arms.

She honked and hissed and flapped her wings and churned her sharp-clawed feet against Stiltskin's arms and stretched out her long neck to press her head against Charming's chest. She looked at him with pleading goose eyes.

I clenched my fists so tight, my fingernails dug holes in my palms. My heart felt as if it had surely torn loose from my chest.

Ulff turned away and covered his eyes with a bristly hand.

"I can't watch," he whispered.

Charming's eyes glistened with tears.

"I'll trade you," he told the peddler. "What is it you want? I'll give you anything."

Stiltskin tried to twist his mouth into his usual horrible smile, but was holding his head back so far to stop his face getting flapped, it ended up an uneasy grimace.

"This goose"—he ducked a wing—"is my golden ticket. She's not for trade."

"Yes," I said. "She is." I took a step toward him.

Stiltskin turned to look at me.

I held my ground.

"You said it yourself," I told him. "In the shoemaker's shop. Everything is for sale or trade."

Now the awful smile did twist Stiltskin's mouth.

"I did indeed," he said.

He turned back to Charming.

"Fine," he said. "What is it you have to trade with me?"

Charming's eyes grew wide. He shot a panicked look at me.

I felt for the pouch under my tunic.

A coin, I mouthed to him.

He nodded. And turned back to Stiltskin.

"A coin," he said.

Stiltskin wrangled one of Marge's clawing feet from his sleeve. And gave Charming a disappointed sigh.

The prince looked at me. I mouthed again.

He turned back.

"A *pouch* of coins," he said.

Stiltskin ducked a lunge of Marge's beak and rolled his eyes at the prince.

"A ring?" said Charming.

"Afraid not."

"A pendant?"

"No."

"A trinket, a bauble, a bead?"

Stiltskin shook his head.

"A plume then!" said Charming. "You once traded information for my plume."

Stiltskin flicked a glance at Charming's helmet.

"I've seen your plume of late," he said. "I think not."

"But there must be *something* you want," said Charming.

"Yes," said Stiltskin.

He wrangled open the cage with one hand and stuffed Marge inside with the other.

"As I told you, I wanted a golden ticket. And now," he said, "I have it."

He bolted the cage shut and picked it up in one hand. It dangled from his gnarled fingers. Inside, Marge flapped and clawed and thrust her head and neck through the bars, reaching, straining for Charming.

The prince held a hand out to her, but Stiltskin jerked the cage from his grasp. It—and Marge—swung wildly from side to side.

A trumpet sounded from the tournament grounds.

"Ah. Just in time." Stiltskin glanced at the king's pennants, fluttering above the arena. "I believe my goose and I shall enjoy a bit of jousting."

24

A Man in a Cloak

Honk!"

Marge plunged her head through the bars of the cage.

The prince stepped toward her, but Stiltskin held him off with a gnarled hand. He swung the cage over the side of the cart and onto the seat.

"HONK!"

Marge scrabbled her webbed goose feet to keep from toppling onto her round goose belly. She flung her head about wildly, looking for Charming.

Ulff clutched at me, his fingers digging into my arm.

I closed my eyes. I couldn't watch.

"Wait!"

A voice rang out.

I snapped open my eyes.

Stiltskin had started to climb onto the cart. He threw a dark glance over his shoulder, and for a whisker of a second, his eyes grew wide. Then they narrowed.

It was the hooded old man from the village, hobbling at a fast limp over the embankment.

I frowned. I'd never seen this man in Twigg before, and all of a sudden, he seemed to pop up everywhere we turned.

He staggered to the back of the cart and stopped, hands on his knees, gasping for air.

"Stop! You can't"—he gulped in a breath—"go."

"Huh," Ulff murmured. "He doesn't *sound* much like a hobbly old man."

He didn't at that. He was out of breath, his voice rasping. He'd most likely run all the way from Twigg. But even raspy, the voice was high-pitched and sweet—too sweet to come from an old man's lips.

"You have my letter," he said.

He straightened then, and the hood slipped from his face. A tumble of hair spilled out.

Charming gasped.

I stared.

"Huh," said Ulff. "He doesn't *look* much like a hobbly old man, either."

He did not.

For he was a she, and she was neither hobbly nor old.

She was the mysterious maiden, the widow's scullery maid.

Cinderella.

My mouth must have dropped open, for I struggled to close it now. I peered at the maiden—

—and saw that she'd fashioned her disguise from the missing things from the library: On her back was Gert's cloak, hiked up and fastened with the man's belt to stop it dragging the ground; on one foot was the boy's boot; and on the other, the lady's buckled shoe. Small wonder she hobbled. She stood before us, cheeks pink from the scrabble up the hill, breath coming out in gasps.

Charming blinked.

"It's . . . you," he said. "We've been looking for you since you ran from the ball."

"Looks like we found her," said Ulff.

"Actually," I said, "she found us."

"My apologies, your highness." Cinderella lowered her head. "I shouldn't have run out. I—I had to get back before my step-, uh, mistress came home."

"Step-mistress?" Ulff frowned and scratched his head. "Well, you're her step-scullery maid, so I guess that makes sense."

I narrowed my eyes. I wasn't sure it made sense at all.

Cinderella turned to Stiltskin.

"Please," she begged him. "You got your goose back."

"Ah." Stiltskin clucked his tongue. "But *you* did not get her for me."

"But you *have* her," she said. "And you've no use for the letter, while it means everything to me."

But Stiltskin only gave a sad shake of his head. "We made a bargain. You promised to retrieve my goose, and I promised that once you did, I would give you the letter."

"He wouldn't," muttered Ulff. "He'd find some way to weasel out."

"If there even *was* a letter," I muttered back. "He likely made the whole thing up."

"I gave you every opportunity," Stiltskin told Cinderella. "But"—he raised his shoulders—"at last, I had to get the goose back myself. The bargain is broken."

He turned and climbed into his cart.

Cinderella stumbled back.

Stiltskin took up the reins, shook them, shook them

192

again, hissed a curse at his mule, and shook them a third time. At last the mule took a step, then another, and peddler and cart trundled away.

Cinderella sank to the ground.

Charming, watching Marge go, nearly sank with her.

"I've lost everything," Cinderella whispered.

"Yes," said Charming.

He let out a long, shuddering sigh.

Then he turned to Cinderella. And frowned.

"Is that Gert's cloak?" he said.

Cinderella glanced down at her clothing. She swallowed and nodded.

"You must think me horrid," she told him.

"I . . . wouldn't say that," said Charming. "Horrid is a strong word. But what is this letter you wanted from Stiltskin?"

She blew out a breath. "It was a letter he said would prove who I was."

I thought back to what the Widow Hedwig had said about her, about the stories the widow claimed she made up.

"Someone with noble ancestors?" I said.

Ulff's eyes grew wide. "And riches in waiting!"

Cinderella nodded. "Hedwig said if I told anyone

who I was, they would never believe me. They'd only laugh, which would be an embarrassment to her, and she'd have to throw me out. I have nowhere else to go, so I've stayed quiet all these long years."

Charming narrowed his eyes. "Until Rumpelstiltskin came along."

"Offering to be your fairy godmother!" said Ulff. He shuddered. "Worst godmother ever."

"You've no idea." Cinderella sighed. "At first it seemed we could be of help to each other. He'd lost his goose at the castle. The ball was the best chance to get her back, but he was banned and needed me to go in his stead. He gave me a gown, a wrap, a pair of shoes, and a carriage to the ball—which turned out to be his rickety old cart."

"The jangle!" I said. "It was the cart we heard in the distance when we found the shoe."

Cinderella nodded. "In return for getting me into the ball—and for the letter he promised—I had to retrieve his goose. And feed her those awful beans. They're supposed to have something in them to make her especially valuable. Vitamins or something." She shrugged. "It seemed a good plan at the time."

"And you wanted to get your book back anyway," I said.

"Yes." She let out a breath. "But in the end, I got neither. The clock struck midnight, and I had to race out. I did manage to sneak back into the castle the next morning. But book and goose were gone."

"So you took the cloak and things"—I waved a hand at her clothing—"as a disguise."

"It's a good one," said Ulff. He nodded, then stopped. "And you've been following us around in it since!"

She nodded. "Little good it did me. And I've been gone so long from the widow's house now, I doubt Hedwig will let me come back." She dropped her head. "I had so very little, and I've lost it all."

"Worry not." Charming leaned down to pat her shoulder. "I shall speak to Thistlewick. Surely, in a place as big as the castle, he can find a position for you. I will tell him what magic you worked with the lost and found."

She looked up. Tears glistened her eyes. "Truly?" She ran the sleeve of Gert's cloak across her nose. "I would be grateful."

She looked grateful. Cleaning the castle wasn't the same as finding a family and the riches. But I'd known a life of sleeping on a hard floor, and I'd known life in the castle. It didn't take me long to get used to a warm bed in a quiet chamber without my brothers snoring above my head. *I* was certainly grateful.

But I glanced at her again as she studied the tournament grounds below. She did look grateful . . . and something else as well. It was in the set of her jaw and lift of her chin. Determined. She looked determined.

A trumpet blared once more.

I looked at Ulff. He looked at me. We both looked at Charming.

Ulff jiggled a hand at him as if jiggling a bit of cloth. I tipped my head toward Cinderella.

Charming closed his eyes for a moment, then turned back to her.

"Apologies, my fine young, er, Cinderella," he said. "I know this is a difficult moment for you, but—"

He flicked a glance at Ulff and me. We nodded.

He cleared his throat. "But speaking of lost things, could you perhaps, if it's at all possible, if you in fact have it with you, return the handkerchief I lent you at the ball?"

Cinderella looked up, eyes glistening with tears. "The . . . what?" She frowned.

"Handkerchief," said Charming. "Hanky. Pocket square. A fine small cloth with embroidery and a bit of lace." Charming jiggled his hand much as Ulff had.

"I know what a handkerchief is," said Cinderella.

"But I don't have one, yours or anyone else's."

Charming stared at her, then at us, panic setting into his eyes.

He turned back to her.

"But you *must* have," he said. "I—I thrust it in your hand. In the library. When Ulff spilled punch down your gown."

"No." Cinderella shook her head. "You gave me this."

She reached inside the cloak and pulled from it a cap. It was battered, made of felt, and covered in punch stains.

Charming took it. "*This* is what I gave you?"

She nodded.

The prince turned it over in his hands.

"This was my lucky cap," he said. "Briefly."

Cinderella wrinkled her brow. "Truly?" she said. "It brought *me* no luck."

"Nor me." Charming let out a breath. His shoulders slumped. "And if you don't have my hanky, I've no chance of luck at all."

The trumpet sounded again.

Ulff and I looked at each other.

Ulff swallowed. "You don't need luck, your highness. You have skill. And armor."

Charming only stared into the distance.

197

"Sir Hugo will have it shined and ready," I told him. "The tournament will begin soon. You can't disappoint your father."

Charming still stared across the embankment.

"I'm afraid I've already disappointed my father," he said.

He waved a hand.

Ulff and I turned to look.

At the top of the hill was the rider in black. He sat tall astride his sleek black steed, the magnificent plume of his helmet rippling in the breeze. He reared his horse, then spurred him toward the tournament grounds.

As they galloped away, Charming dropped his head. He stared at the stained felt cap in his hands. I reached across to pat his shoulder.

An entire fanfare of trumpets blared across the castle grounds.

Charming and I paid little attention.

But Ulff glanced up.

Then straightened.

Then grabbed my arm and nearly shook it from my shoulder.

"Look!" He pointed.

Charming and I followed his gaze. The black-armored rider was still galloping toward the tournament grounds.

But beyond him, entering the arena itself, led by a line of trumpeters and a company of the king's men—

—was his majesty the king, Charming's father, wearing his most royal of robes and carrying his royal scepter.

I leaned forward and narrowed my eyes to be sure he *was* the king.

But there was no mistaking his steady stride as he wound his way through the cheering crowd. Angelica trotted at his side, waving to the people and scooping up the flowers they tossed at her. Behind them marched the king's advisors and another company of the king's men. They made their way across the arena and up the steps to the king's royal box. His majesty turned then and waved.

Charming stared. He looked from the king to the black-armored rider and back again. His face creased in confusion.

"But . . . if the rider isn't my father," he said, "who is he?"

Ulff narrowed his eyes. He studied the arena, his eyes scanning the king's box and surrounding seats.

"I don't know," he said. "But has anyone seen that blackhearted knave, Sir Roderick?"

25

A Sly Bit of Trickery

Jhad no idea, your highness."

Sir Hugo hoisted the gleaming breastplate over Charming's shoulders. It cast a glimmer through the shadows of the stable.

"I thought he was the king. I swear I did." He moved to the back to pull the leather straps of the breastplate tight. "He was surely wearing the king's armor. I had no thought he was that mangy ditch worm, Sir Roderick"— Sir Hugo's mouth twisted like he'd *swallowed* a mangy ditch worm—"else I'd have never let him near the royal training grounds. I swear it."

He buckled the straps, then circled to the front to shift the breastplate in place. At last, he looked up. He took a long, shuddering breath, his eyes pleading for forgiveness.

Charming placed a hand on Sir Hugo's shoulder. "I've known you the whole of my life, good sir," he said. "I would never doubt your loyalty, nor your honor. As for Sir Roderick—" His mouth clenched in a firm line. "He must have taken, er, borrowed, er—"

"Stolen, more like," muttered Ulff.

"—my father's armor."

Sir Hugo nodded. "That would be my guess." He turned toward the trestle table set up outside Darnell's stall.

Sir Hugo had spent the morning burnishing Charming's armor to a glassy sheen, then laid out the pieces on the table in the order he would harness them onto the prince.

Now he lifted the prince's backplate. Charming stood with his arms out so Sir Hugo could fit it to him. Ulff and I plucked up his arm bracers and pauldrons— the shoulder guards—and held them at the ready. As I passed a bracer to Sir Hugo, I caught the prince flicking a glance to the side, toward the spot where Marge should have been stalking about, keeping guard with raised wings and a sharp hiss.

Charming swallowed and flicked his glance away. His goose was not with us.

Nor was Cinderella.

I handed Sir Hugo a pauldron.

The scullery maid had told us she had unfinished business. She had promised to return the cloak to Charming—for he had himself had promised to return it to Gert—and slipped away, pulling the hood up over her head.

"Almost there, your highness." Sir Hugo slid the last bit of armor in place—the prince's gauntlets.

Charming stretched and clenched his armored fists. Then he gathered Darnell's reins and led the steadfast steed clopping from the cool darkness of the stables into the brilliant sun of the tournament grounds.

The grandstand stood tall over the tiltyard. Flags fluttered atop its poles. Colorful bunting was draped over the length of it. Twigg folk, as well as folk from farms and villages near and far, were packed into the stands. The railings fairly groaned from the weight of them. Children were tucked on laps and hefted onto shoulders, some dangling from the sides of the grandstand itself.

Those who couldn't find seats pushed in along the

fence that surrounded the tiltyard, some standing, some sitting on barrels and overturned crates, plus one girl on a tuffet. The boy Jack was with his milk cow, and a few people were in carts. Beyond them, large colorful tents ruffled in the breeze—the pavilions of the visiting jousters.

But something tugged my attention back to the carts at the fence.

I looked closer.

And blinked in surprise. For one of those carts—the one far from other spectators—was a dung cart. Over the sides of it sprawled a pack of Swills: my father and my three brothers. Gerald rubbed his eyes. Lout yawned so wide, I couldn't make out his face. And Snout looked to have fallen asleep entirely—until my father shoved his shoulder, jolting him awake. I couldn't blame them. They farmed the dung at night. On any other day, this would be their prime sleeping hour.

What surprised me was the bubble of joy that rose in my chest at seeing them. Not that I wanted to go back to a life of ducking their fists or sleeping with Gerald's boot for a pillow. But (save shoving each others' faces into the dung) Swill life held little in the way of entertainment. I was glad the king had made sure to invite them.

My glance fell on another cart. It was closer, wedged in behind the crowd at the fence.

It was the peddler's cart. On the seat sat Rumpelstiltskin, trying to force one of his cursed blue beans through the bars of the cage beside him. And was that—

I peered closer.

—a hunched man in a hooded cloak lurking behind the cart?

I cast a glance at Charming, but he seemed not to notice peddler nor cage. Nor the hunched man who looked suspiciously like Cinderella in Gert's cloak.

I was glad of it.

In the middle of the grandstand sat the king in his royal box, draped in robes and surrounded by advisors and the lords and ladies of the court. On his one side sat Princess Angelica, fairly bouncing in her seat.

On his other side, the seat was empty.

As I watched, the king turned toward the empty seat. He studied it for a moment, then turned to survey the cluster of jousters lining up at the far end of the tiltyard. At the end of the line, apart from the others, was the rider in black. The king crossed his arms and sat back in his throne, and even from this great distance,

I could near feel the heat burning from his anger.

This, Charming *did* see. And his anger burned equally hot.

Sir Roderick had pulled off a sly bit of trickery. He had much the same build as the king. Outfitted in the king's well-known black armor, astride a horse the exact match of the king's famed black warhorse, anyone would think he *was* the king. His majesty himself might well think he was looking in a mirror.

But as I watched Prince Charming, I couldn't but think that in the end, the trick might be on Sir Roderick.

The prince cast one last burning look at Roderick. Then, before Ulff and I and Sir Hugo knew to take our places to boost him up or catch him as he fell, he thrust a foot in Darnell's stirrup and, in one flawless move, swung his other leg over his steed's back. He settled into the saddle, straight and true. And facing the right direction.

Ulff looked at me, eyebrows near flying from his forehead. I looked back, my eyebrows in pure agreement.

For seated there, astride Darnell, sun glinting off his armor, our prince looked the match of any champion in the long row of portraits in the library.

His jaw was clenched, his chin lifted high. His

shoulders, which displayed excellent posture even in his lowest of moments, were held so broad and square they looked to be carved of stone. Sir Hugo had re-feathered his helmet, and now his plume stood straight and tall and plumy, rippling atop his head. Darnell, too, seemed fiercer, his flank draped in a magnificent caparison, his face protected by his own gleaming chanfron.

A chorus of trumpets blasted a fanfare over the arena. Charming snapped a quick dip of his head toward Sir Hugo, Ulff, and me, and spurred Darnell off to join the parade of jousters.

As I watched him, my breath caught in my chest. Not because Charming looked valiant. For Charming always looked valiant. In truth, he never looked *more* valiant than in the moment before he marched straight into a tree branch and flipped onto his backplate like a beetle.

But he did not always hold the same fire. As he gazed across the tournament grounds now, Charming's eyes were two coals smoldering with flame.

I swallowed. For the prince would need every bit of that fire to win the joust and save the tournament cup from Sir Roderick.

26

A Prince at the Tilt

Sir Hugo scrambled to take his spot with the other knight's squires. Ulff and I scuttled across the tiltyard toward the grandstand.

As we climbed the steps, I saw that sheets of parchment had been hammered to the posts. I looked closer. They were rules of the joust. I stopped for a moment, for I'd not yet seen a true joust, only Charming's training.

Rules of the Joust

1. For each round, jousters will make three passes.
2. Jousters will score points on each pass:

   Miss: 0 points and complete humiliation

   Hit: 1 point

   Hit + broken lance tip: 2 points

   Hit + shattered lance: 3 points

3. At the end of three passes, the jouster with the most points wins and moves to the next round. The jouster with fewer points must admit defeat, for he is out of the tournament.

4. If a jouster unhorses his opponent, he is immediately declared the winner and moves on to the next round. Unhorsed jousters shall rub their wounds, nurse their broken pride, and admit defeat, for they are out of the tournament.

5. Jousters shall not strike their opponents below the shield nor strike their opponent's horse with any part of their lance nor armor. Competitors breaking these rules should be ashamed to call themselves jousters, and in fact, should only call themselves spectators, for they are out of the tournament.

I'd scarce finished scanning the rules before Ulff grasped my arm and pulled me after him.

We wedged our way through the crowd to the king's royal box.

Angelica patted the seats she'd saved for us on the bench next to her.

"I feared you wouldn't make it," she whispered.

"I feared it myself," said Ulff.

As we squeezed in, trumpets blasted once more. The jousters paraded past the stands, Charming leading the way, plume pluming, Darnell's caparison flowing. Roderick, in black, brought up the rear. The crowd cheered and stomped and clapped.

As the jousters paraded off, the tournament crier strode to the center of the list. He carried a parchment scroll before him.

A hush fell over the grandstand.

The crier unscrolled the scroll.

"The first contest," cried the crier, "is between Sir Wendell of Wimberley and—"

Ulff and Angelica and I leaned forward, along with the king and his advisors and the lords and ladies and everyone in the stands and surrounding grounds.

"—Sir Haggis MacDonald," cried the crier.

"Oh!" A surprised murmur rippled through the crowd.

Ulff frowned. "Is that bad?"

I raised my shoulders in a shrug.

But the king tipped his head toward the tiltyard.

At one end, a slight knight on a fine-boned horse: Sir Wendell of Wimberley.

214

At the other, a strapping rider on a strapping steed, so strapping that jouster's armor and horse's caparison both strained over the sheer strappingness of them: Sir Haggis MacDonald.

"Hardly seems a fair fight," said Ulff.

"Hardly seems a fight at all," said the king.

The tournament master dropped his flag. Sir Wendell and Sir Haggis spurred their horses.

Sir Wendell had barely time to lower his lance when—

Thhhhhunkkkkk.

Sir Haggis's lance cudgeled him square in the shield, flipping him backward from his fine-boned horse.

"Huh." Ulff blinked. "That took less time than I would've thought. At this rate, the whole thing'll be over afore I get my seat warmed good."

Sir Wendell of Wimberley lay sprawled where he'd fallen. Haggis MacDonald rode to his side, leaned over, and with one massive gauntleted hand, lifted Wendell from the straw. He raised Sir Wendell's visor and peered inside.

He turned to the grandstand. "Still breathing!" he called.

The crowd cheered. Sir Haggis tucked Sir Wendell under his arm and rode off.

We watched three rounds after that, most of them more equally matched than Haggis and Wendell, though Sir Roderick made quick work of his first opponent, a young knight jousting in his first tournament.

Because he was Roderick, he made a lopsided fight even more uneven, unhorsing the knight by, in a way, unhorsing the horse. As Roderick charged down the list, he trained his lance square on the horse's face. When the horse stuttered in his step, the young knight sat upright. Roderick swung up his lance and pummeled the knight's shield, knocking the knight from his saddle.

It was not against the rules, for he never touched the horse. But the crowd booed and banged their fists on the stands and threw shoes and half-eaten turkey legs at Roderick's head.

"Scab-cankered varlet," muttered Ulff.

"Yes," the king murmured.

As Roderick rode off, the crier strode onto the list once more.

"The next contest," cried the crier, "is between Prince Charming—"

Ulff dug his fingers into my one arm, Angelica my other. I scarce felt them, for I was digging my own fingers into my knees.

"—and Sir Gawain of Grimm."

Sir Gawain of Grimm? Ulff and I looked at each other. We'd neither of us heard the name before.

Sir Gawain turned out to be a fearsome fellow, nimble with his lance, a swagger in his bearing. His well-muscled and equally swaggering steed pulled at the bit, ready to charge.

Sir Gawain and Charming lined up at opposite ends of the tilt. They held their wooden lances upright and leaned forward, tensed for the ride.

The tournament master lifted his flag.

I scarce breathed. I may have blacked out for a moment. When I came to, Sir Gawain and Prince Charming were thundering toward each other, lances to the fore. Charming leaned in, focused. As did Sir Gawain. As they approached each other, Charming thrust his lance, striking Gawain's shield—

—at the exact moment Gawain struck Charming's.

"One hit for each," said Angelica. "They're tied at a point apiece."

I collapsed back in my seat.

The jousters trotted back to the ends of the list and lined up once more, lances at the ready, horses blowing out heavy breaths. The tournament master dropped his flag. Charming and Gawain spurred their horses to a gallop.

And each hit the other's shield, square and true.

But as Sir Gawain's lance swept away clean, Charming's shattered in a shower of bits.

The crowd cheered.

Ulff leaned forward, gripping the rail.

"No!" he moaned. "The prince broke his lance."

"That's a good thing," Angelica told him.

I tipped my head toward the sheet of parchment—the rules of the joust— nailed to the corner of the royal box.

Ulff frowned. He glanced about to make sure no one was watching, then reached into his lumpy leather cap and pulled out his eyeglasses. He slid them on and peered at the paper.

I could tell when he got to the scoring part, and the line "Hit + shattered lance," for I saw him mouth the words *three points*.

"Ho!" Ulff threw his fist in the air. "The prince broke his lance!"

He sat back and slipped his glasses under his cap.

Sir Hugo scuttled out onto the tiltyard to hand the prince a new lance, and the jousters edged up to their starting points. Sir Gawain and his charger stared down the list. Charming lifted his chin. Darnell tossed his head and snorted.

The master dropped the flag. Jousters charged, closer, and closer still. Charming held steady, focused on his target.

Sir Gawain thrust first, lance tip aimed straight at Charming's shield.

But Charming struck it away as he rammed the tip of his own lance into Gawain's shield.

The hit struck true. Gawain pitched sideways, in slow motion, it seemed. His arms swung around, his legs flew loose from the stirrups.

And Sir Gawain of Grimm plummeted to the straw.

He lay there a moment. The crowd went silent.

Then he sat up, shook his head—shaking the sense back into it, most like—and climbed to his feet.

"Huzzah!" the crowd cheered, seeing him stand unharmed.

After defeating Sir Gawain of Grimm, the prince's

confidence was higher than I'd ever seen in him. Over his next three contests, he faced three of the tournament's best jousters—Lord William of Braversham, Sir Roger Thatch, and Angus the Axhearted.

But he neither stumbled nor flinched. Leaning forward, lance steady, plume full, he scored nine hits, breaking three tips, shattering six lances, and unhorsing all three.

As Angus the Axhearted hit the straw, his heavy *clank* echoing through the arena, the crowd leapt to its feet. They stomped and cheered and chanted the prince's name.

Charming turned to them, bowed his head, and tipped his lance.

"Huzzah!"

The prince turned again, this time to face the only other jouster still standing, the only other jouster to defeat each of his previous opponents.

The rider in black.

The scoundrel who'd stolen the king's own armor.

The mangy, black-knaved wretch himself.

Sir Roderick.

27

A Joust Down to Two

The crier stepped to the center of the tilt. A hush fell over the grounds.

"In the final matchup," cried the crier, reading from his scroll, "to determine the champion of the joust, winner of the tournament, conqueror of the cup, and hero of the realm—"

We leaned forward, waiting, though we well knew what the crier would cry.

"—Sir Roderick on one side, competing in fierce battle against—"

The crowd drew a tense breath.

"—His Royal Highness, Prince Charming of Twigg."

The crowd erupted in cheers.

And it was plain they'd picked a favorite.

A trumpet blared, and Sir Roderick rode to his starting spot at one end of the tilt, visor raised. His black armor glowed with a dark sheen that seemed to suck the very sunlight from the sky, and he tipped his chin so low, his black plume looked more a threat than a decoration. His black charger huffed and reared his head and pawed the ground.

The spectators clapped. Politely. But here and there throughout the stands—and even more so amongst folk pressed against the fence—a few hisses escaped.

Sir Roderick turned on them with a dark scowl. The hissers gulped back their hisses.

The trumpet blared once more, and Prince Charming rode to the list.

His armor glinted rays of light. His plume swayed in a billowy wave. Darnell held his head high. His chanfron, too, glinted sunlight.

The crowd cheered. Not politely, like with Sir Roderick. Full-throated and thundering, as spectators tossed streamers onto the tiltyard and joggled babies in the air. Ulff and Angelica and I and the advisors and lords and ladies leapt to our feet, clapping. The king leaned forward, hands gripping the arms of his throne.

His whole face was a beaming smile.

Charming turned to the crowd, just as Sir Roderick had. But he cast no scowl, for Charming had no scowl within him to cast. He simply placed one gauntleted palm over his heart and bowed his head.

The cheers grew more thunderous. The stomps quaked the stands till I thought the planks under our feet would give way.

I glanced down the length of the tiltyard—and caught Sir Roderick casting another look, this time at Charming. It was a look so filled with venom, for a moment, I feared it could unhorse the prince from the sheer force of its scorn.

The tournament master strode onto the list. The crowd hushed. Charming and Roderick rattled shut their visors and took firm grip of their lances, holding them upright, at the ready.

Ulff, Angelica, and I clutched the rail.

The master dropped the flag, and the jousters spurred their horses. They tore down the list, plumes swept back, caparisons lashing over their horses' flanks.

Clackkkk.

Clackkkk.

One lance hit at near the same instant as the other.

Roderick's was a solid strike—

—but Charming's splintered the end of his lance. The tip broke free and hurtled over the tiltyard.

"Huzzah!" cried the crowd.

"Yes!" Angelica threw her fists in the air. "A hit for Sir Roderick. A tip break for Charming. Charming's ahead, two points to one."

I stole a look across the tiltyard at the dung cart. My father and brothers were fully awake now, hammering their fists in the air and whooping.

My heart swelled seeing them cheer for the prince. As contrary as they were, I half worried they'd be in Sir Roderick's corner. Or worse, some of them in Roderick's,

the others in the prince's, ending in a fistfight right here on the castle grounds.

My glance circled to the peddler's cart. Stiltskin was not cheering. But he gave all his attention to the excitement on the list. And little of it to the goose in the cage beside him.

But someone else assuredly did.

Someone who looked like a hunched man in a hooded cloak. Someone who had edged up to the side of the cart and was eyeing the cage.

Ulff dug an elbow into my ribs, and I pulled my gaze back to the tiltyard.

Charming and Roderick had circled their horses

back to their starting spots. Charming held a new lance, its tip attached. Roderick lowered his head and fixed a stare down the tiltyard at the prince.

The master dropped the flag. The jousters charged.

Charming lowered his lance, training it on Sir Roderick. Roderick lowered his lance at the same time.

But he did not train it on Charming.

He trained it on Darnell. Particularly, Darnell's head.

"Muck-breath churl!" cried Ulff. "It's the same trick he used on that young knight!"

But Charming was not the young knight, and Darnell was not the young knight's horse. As Charming held his lance steady, Darnell thundered on without a flicker of eyelash nor stammer of hoof. At the last moment, Roderick raised his lance and thrust it at Charming's shield.

Clanngggk.

Clanngggk.

This time, it was Roderick who scored a broken tip.

But Charming's lance shattered completely into a shower of chunks.

Three more points for Charming. For Sir Roderick, only two.

"A hit and a tip break." Ulff counted his fingers. "A tip break and a shattered lance—" He looked down at his hands. He was running out of fingers.

"Five to three!" Angelica clenched her fists. "He can do this! He can *really* do this!"

Again the jousters circled to their ends of the tilt, steam rising from the heavy breaths of the horses.

At the tournament master's signal, they set off, thundering toward each other, Charming never wavering, never slowing down.

But as they drew closer, Roderick reached into his gauntlet and pulled out a bit of cloth.

I leaned forward, squinting at Roderick's armored hand.

And froze. Beside me, Ulff sucked in a breath.

I reached for Ulff's arm. "He's got—"

"The hanky!" Ulff grabbed my arm back. "That viper's got his flea-rotted hands on the prince's hanky."

Roderick held the hanky above his head. It whipped and flapped like a lace-trimmed banner.

I shook my head. *How* had he gotten his flea-rotted hands on it?

I thought back to the night of the ball. And blinked.

When the clock had struck midnight, Charming had run out of the library after Cinderella—and hurled headlong into Roderick.

"That's when it happened!" I said. "When Charming was chasing after Cinderella and bumped into Sir Roderick, Roderick plucked the hanky right from the prince's gauntlet."

Sir Roderick swung the hanky overhead, as if swinging a lasso, slowly at first, then faster and faster still, till he let loose and flung the hanky into the wind ahead of him. It floated for a moment, then fluttered to the dirt of the tiltyard.

Charming sat up in his saddle, just a bit, and just for a moment. The tip of his lance, until then straight and true, bobbled just the slightest. Darnell's hoofbeats stuttered just the tiniest.

Then Charming leaned forward, steadied his lance, and dug his heels into Darnell's sides. Darnell picked up speed, his hooves grinding over grass and earth.

But in that instant, a honk rang out. I glanced around to see Marge flap over the fence and waddle straight for the jousting course—

—and the hanky.

28

A Goose on the Tiltyard

With wings held high, Marge flap-dawdled onto the list. Her long neck was stretched forward. Her goose eyes were trained on the hanky. She plucked it up in her bill and turned toward Charming—

—straight into the path of Darnell's thundering hooves.

"Marge!" cried Angelica.

"She'll be crushed!" cried Ulff.

"Nooooooo!" cried I.

The crowd gasped.

Ulff grabbed my arm. I grabbed his back.

And shot a glance at the peddler's cart.

Stiltskin was staring at the empty cage beside him, its door swung open.

233

Beside the cart, the hunched man clutched the fence. The hood of the cloak had slipped back, and beneath it, Cinderella's face was an anguished twist.

"I'll get her!" a voice shouted.

I turned to see Angelica pulling up her skirts. She gripped the rail at the front of the royal box, aiming to swing over into the tiltyard. But the king seized the back of her gown and pulled her back.

Down on the list, Charming lifted his head from the gallop.

But only for a flash.

Then he leaned into it again and flipped his lance under his arm.

Marge had stopped in her waddle and now let out a squawking hiss.

But the prince did not flinch. Nor did his horse. As they galloped alongside the goose, Charming swooped down, plucked her from the dirt, and placed her in front of him on his saddle.

Sir Roderick's terrible laugh rang out above the pounding of hooves. He trained his lance on Charming, steady and deadly.

Charming had no chance. In moments, he'd be hit, he and the goose both thrust from his horse.

But in the flick of an eyelash, Charming flipped his lance from arm to hand and, still clutching Marge tight, thrust it forward.

CLAANNGGGK!

He struck Sir Roderick in the chest plate, square and true.

"Oooof!"

Roderick's groan echoed over the tiltyard.

He lurched back, lance flying behind him, his body wrenched from the saddle.

As his horse charged ahead, Roderick plunged backward through empty space, as if in slow motion, arms windmilling, legs sprawled, until—

Clunngggk.

Thunnnggk.

—he crashed into the hoof-packed dirt of the tiltyard.

29

A Vase for a Churl

HUZZAH!"

The crowd cheered and tossed at Charming whatever they happened to hold in their hands—flowers and flags and ribbons and bits of colored paper and sweet rolls and a baby's rattle—until Darnell, Charming, and Marge stood hoof deep in it.

Ulff, Angelica, and I—and even the stodgy advisors and very proper lords and ladies behind us—leapt to our feet.

Angelica gripped my arm and gave it a joyous shake. Ulff balled his hand into a fist and gave my other arm a cheerful punch. Both my arms grew numb from it, but I little

cared. I tore the list of jousting rules from the corner of
the royal box and shredded it, tossing the pieces in the
air.

The king leaned forward, eyes gleaming. He was
tempted to leap and cheer, too. I could tell by the way
he gripped the arm of his throne.

Instead, he thumped his royal scepter against the
planks under his feet and murmured, "Well done, son.
Well done."

The tournament master strode across the tiltyard
one last time. The crier followed, scroll at the ready.

Behind them marched a pair of the king's men,
carrying before them the enormous tournament cup.
Sunlight glinted off the gold, nearly blinding the crowd.
Thistlewick had clearly been busy with his polishing
rag.

The king rose then and made his way down to
the tiltyard. Angelica followed, grabbing my arm and
dragging me along. I poked Ulff and tipped my head,
and he trotted to catch up.

When the king had reached the tiltyard, and servants
had scrambled to arrange his robes royally about him,
a trumpeter blasted out a flourish. The cheers of the
crowd dwindled to a hush, save a stray whistle here
and there.

Charming stood before his father, holding Darnell's bridle in one hand, clutching Marge to his chest with the other. He'd pulled off his helmet, and his hair stood up at odd, sweat-soaked angles. His face was flushed pink.

Still, his eyes shone—with pride, I think. And honor.

Sir Roderick's eyes shone, too. But with neither pride nor honor. He stood off to one side, huffing out impatient breaths, his glare burning a hole of fury through Charming.

The crier unscrolled his scroll.

"His royal majesty the king," cried the crier, "will award the second-place trophy to the most honorable Sir Roderick."

"Honorable." Ulff snorted. "Huh."

A second pair of king's men I hadn't before noticed stepped forward. They carried between them a smaller cup. They presented it to the king.

I leaned in for a better look. It wasn't a cup so much as a vase, and it did seem small next to the enormous gold tournament cup.

But by itself, it was a thing to behold—glimmering silver with swirling handles. It would be the find of a lifetime if I'd scooped something like it from the dung pit.

Sir Roderick eyed it as if it *were* the dung pit.

The king held it out to him. "Sir Roderick, you rode valiantly and well. I am pleased to bestow upon you—"

"Yes, yes. Thank you, it's an honor, and all that." Roderick snatched the vase from the king's hand and stalked off, leading his gleaming black steed behind him.

The crowd booed and tossed watermelon rinds.

The king watched him go.

He sighed. "Roderick *is* consistent, I'll give him that. He hasn't much changed since our days together in the tournament."

Angelica looked up. "Sir Roderick competed when *you* won the tournament?"

The king nodded. "And acted much the same then as he did now at being awarded second place."

240

Second place then *and* now? I turned to stare at Sir Roderick, or rather, at Sir Roderick's back as he strode from the arena, the silver cup dangling from his hand, a chunk of watermelon stuck to his spur. He'd lost once to the king, and once more to the king's son.

"Half explains why he's so churlish," Ulff muttered.

I nodded. "Part of me almost feels sorry for him."

"Almost," said Ulff.

The crier tucked the first scroll under his arm and unfurled a second. The first pair of king's men stepped forward, wielding the enormous gold cup, and presented it to the king.

"And now," cried the crier, "the moment we've been waiting for. His royal majesty the king will award the first-place tournament cup to the champion of the joust, winner of the tournament, conqueror of the cup, and hero of the realm—"

The crowd erupted.

"—His Royal Highness Prince Charming of Twigg!" the crier cried.

The crowd began chanting the prince's name.

The king held out the cup. "It is a privilege, my son." His chest puffed. His eyes glistened.

Charming bowed his head. "Thank you, Father. It

shall go back to its place of honor in the castle library."

He reached for the cup then, trying to juggle Marge in his one hand and Darnell's bridle in the other. Sir Hugo took the bridle from him, and Ulff reached for the goose.

But Marge was having none of it. She jabbed her bill at him, the hanky she still clutched swatting his cheek. Ulff jumped back.

The prince sighed, lifted Marge into the cup, then took both goose and cup from his father.

The crowd cheered.

"Prince and goose," they chanted. "Prince and goose!"

"Wait just one second!"

A spindly voice rang out, piercing the chants of the crowd.

30

A Prince Finds His Charm

I turned. Stiltskin must have climbed the fence, for now he beetled toward us across the tiltyard, elbows and knees swinging like an angry string puppet. Cinderella hobbled after him in her mismatched boot and shoe, hood swept back, Gert's cloak flying out behind her.

"No, *you* wait one second!"

Another voice rang out, firm and high.

I swiveled my head.

From the other direction marched Cook, *our* cook, the cook from the castle.

She and Stiltskin reached Charming—and the gold cup full of Marge—at the same time.

Cook planted her fists on her considerable hips and leaned toward Stiltskin till their noses nearly touched.

"You were banned," Cook snarled at him.

Stiltskin pulled his head back. "Not from the grounds, madam," he said. "Only from the castle. And not for long, I am certain, once the king has seen what I can do."

"Oh, his majesty is well aware what you can do," said Cook.

But Stiltskin ignored her. He turned to Charming.

"Pardon me, your highness," he said, "but once again, you have my goose."

He reached for the cup, clasping his knobby fingers around one of the golden handles.

"No, sir." Cook slapped his hand away and reached for the cup herself, wrapping both arms around it. "He has *my* goose. The one you thieved from the castle kitchens."

"*Thieved?*" The word rolled in murmurs through the grandstand.

"Oh!" Ulff's eyes popped wide. "*Marge* is why he was banned." He looked at the goose in wonder. "We had her with us all this time and never knew."

Charming's eyes grew narrow. "Thieved?" He stared

at Stiltskin. "You insisted she was yours. You played on my honor. And all the while you had *thieved* her?"

Cinderella's eyes grew even narrower. "And you had me scouring castle and countryside to get her back. You turned *me* into a thief as well."

The crowd booed.

"I—what?—no." Stiltskin held up his hands. "I thieved no goose. And this is not the same goose, in any case. And even if it were, I've been feeding her all these long weeks highly valuable bird feed. You see?" He reached in his pocket and pulled out a handful of the odd blue beans. "I should have some claim to her for my troubles, should I not?"

He pushed Cook away and reached for the cup.

"You've no claim whatsoever," said Charming. He pulled the cup from the both of them and held it firmly to his breastplate. "A thieved goose is a thieved goose, no matter what you've done for her." He shifted the cup in his arms. "Though she does seem well fed."

"But—" Stiltskin swallowed. A lump bobbed in his skinny throat. "You can't. You shan't. I've so much invested. That goose is—"

"Your golden ticket," said Charming. "So you said. But you'll need to find opportunity elsewhere, for Marge is no one's ticket. She's my—my—" He glanced down at her, nesting in the cup. "Well, I'm not sure what she is, but she's no ticket." He turned to Cook. "Nor is she a fixing for your stewpot, dear Cook. My apologies."

"None needed, your highness." Cook patted his armored arm. "I couldn't have gone through with it anyway. She's too fine a bird."

She turned to make her way back to the stands and the other castle servants.

Stiltskin stood where he was, clenching and unclenching his gnarly fists.

"Your highness," he said. His teeth were clenched, too. "Your most royal and, yes, honorable highness. I must beg you to recons—"

A pair of the king's men stepped toward him.

Stiltskin looked up at them and took a step back.

The king cleared his throat. "You are fortunate, Mr. Stiltskin, that I only banned you from the castle. For thieving a goose, I could have banned you from this kingdom, the next kingdom, and many kingdoms beyond." He raised an eyebrow. "It's not too late for me to do so now should I find myself displeased."

Stiltskin gulped, the lump in his skinny neck bobbing. He gave one last longing glance at Marge, a more furtive glance at the king's men, then scarpered off across the tiltyard, knees and elbows waggling.

The crowd jeered. Someone threw a mutton pie at him.

I watched, making sure he was well and truly gone.

He scrambled over the fence and started to climb onto his cart.

Then stopped.

For he'd spied young Jack and his milk cow.

The peddler ambled over and, after a quick, darted glance to see no one was watching, flung an arm around the boy's shoulder. He reached into his pocket and pulled out the handful of beans. He held them up as he spoke quickly in young Jack's ear.

"That can't be good." Ulff tipped his chin in their direction. "Somebody should warn the lad."

I nodded.

"Oh, dear. Look at the smudge."

We turned again.

This time, it was Thistlewick who scurried up. He flicked a cloth from his waistcoat and began rubbing the fingerprints from Charming's gold cup. Marge leaned over the cup's edge and poked her bill at the polishing cloth. Thistlewick brushed her away.

At last, he stood back to examine his work. He gave a sharp nod.

"Good as new," he said.

He tucked the cloth back into his waistcoat, snapped a bow of his head at the king and prince, and turned sharp on his heel to leave.

Then stopped and turned back.

"Your highness." He leaned toward the prince, his voice low. "Speaking of good as new, I've repaired the, uh, book you brought to me. I wasn't sure how urgently you needed it, but I have it with me just in case."

He patted his waistcoat.

"Book?" Cinderella gasped. She turned to Charming. "*My* book?"

"The very one that fell out of your, er, Gert's cloak in the library," said Charming.

He gave a nod to Thistlewick, who pulled the book from an inside pocket. He handed it to the prince.

Charming ran a gauntleted hand over it. Thistlewick had done fine work indeed. The leather of the cover was smooth and no longer goose-chewed. The pages were straight and clean.

The prince turned and handed it to Cinderella.

"Thank you," she whispered. She grasped the book to her chest and closed her eyes. "It's the only thing I have left of my mother. I thought it was gone forever."

The king frowned. "May I see it?"

Cinderella looked up at him. She hesitated, then held out the book.

He took it and gently opened it.

"I recognize this." He pointed to a pair of swirling initials scrawled inside the cover: *QM*. "My wife, the late Queen Matilde, gave it to her dearest friend, the old squire's wife." He looked up. "If this book came from your mother, you, my dear, must be the old squire's daughter."

Cinderella blinked. "I am," she said. "I was. Only, I had no proof. It's why I agreed to help Rumpelstiltskin. He said he'd found a letter that would prove who I was. I'd have had naught to do with him otherwise, the scalawag peddler."

"I doubt he found anything." The king's voice was gentle. "It was likely a ruse to get you doing his bidding. But this"—he handed the book back to her—"is better proof than any scalawag peddler could dig up. It looks to me as if your stepmother and her daughters have cheated from you what is rightfully yours these long years."

The crowd jeered and hissed at that, and a rustle churned up in the center of the stands. It churned to the grandstand steps and cast the Widow Hedwig onto the tiltyard like an enormous, roiling mouth spitting out a bone. Two more bones followed—Elfrida and Gert.

The widow straightened her skirts. She turned to the crowd, then Cinderella.

"I—I—had no idea." Her voice was high and pleading. "I thought the house and everything in it was mine. Truly. I am his widow, after all. How was I to know?"

The crowd booed again and jostled for something left to throw.

The Widow Hedwig ducked a sausage roll, picked up her skirts, and stomped from the arena. Gert and Elfrida scrambled to catch up.

"My cloak!" was the last we heard from any of them as they rounded the grandstand and headed across the grounds. "Mother, my *cloak*!"

"It looks as though that big house is entirely yours now," the king told Cinderella. "Though if you need someone to clean it"—he tipped his head in the direction where the widow and her daughters had disappeared— "those three might need a hearth to sleep on."

Charming shifted the tournament cup to one arm and gently pulled the hanky from Marge's bill. It was dirty and wrinkled and wet with goose spit.

"Forgive me," he told the king. "You trusted this to me, and now"—he held up the limp hanky—"look at the state of it."

"When I gave it to you," said the king, "I knew well what might happen. You were taking it with you to the joust, after all. Your mother knew it, too, when she gave it to me. Besides, Thistlewick will soon have it cleaned and pressed and in fine form."

Charming nodded. "He will at that."

He handed the hanky to Thistlewick, who beamed, folded it into a neat square, and tucked it into his waistcoat.

"But you were right." Charming looked up at his father. "The luck isn't in the charm itself. It's in what the charm means to you."

The king nodded. "It is." He put out his hand and

carefully stroked Marge's head. "And I can see she means a great deal to you."

Charming's eyes opened in surprise. Then he tipped his head and studied the goose.

"She does," he said. "I've rescued her twice now from the joust."

"And hit the target each time, too," said Ulff.

Charming nodded. "She truly does seem to be my lucky charm, doesn't she?"

Marge, who'd been restless since the prince took the hanky from her, now fluttered her tail feathers and raised her wings and let out an annoyed honk.

Charming set the cup down and lifted her from it. The goose wrestled free from him, waddled to a clump of straw, and sat. She gabbled and rustled and wriggled. Then she settled into a roost.

Ulff watched her. His eyebrows popped high. "I think our Marge has laid an egg."

He reached under her rump and pulled out something large and shiny.

"Well, would you look at that," he said. "It's . . . gold." He rapped his knuckles on it. "And solid." His eyes grew wide. *"This!"* He held it up. "It's the *egg* what's the golden ticket."

We all leaned in for a better look.

"Hmmm," said Charming. "This golden ticket seems to have a tinge of blue."

Author's Note
At the Tilt

In *Clocked!*, folks from throughout the kingdom pack into an arena to watch jousters compete in the king's tournament. As the competitors charge toward each other—and the crowd cheers and boos and chucks rotten food—you may have thought, *Hmmm, this seems a lot like a modern sporting event. A football game, maybe. Or a particularly aggressive badminton match.*

And you would be right.

Tournaments were the Super Bowls of the Middle Ages. The best jousters were admired and celebrated like our superstar athletes today.

Tournaments began as a way for knights to practice their battle skills between wars. At first, tournaments looked like actual battles, with two teams fighting each other in a free-for-all, trying to capture opposing knights that they could later ransom for money. This was called a "melee" (pronounced may-lay), from a French word that means "mixture." Today, we still use the word melee to describe a wild, mixed-up skirmish.

Over time, tournaments evolved, and jousting became

the most popular event. Tournament winners could take home quite a haul of money, jewels, and sometimes land and noble titles. In some tournaments, the winner could even take their opponent's armor and horse. These riches were tempting, and—just as in *Clocked!*—some jousters resorted to cheating, most often by bolting their armor to their horse's saddle so they could not be unhorsed.

As jousting became more popular, competitors tried to make it safer. They wore special, protective armor and used lances with blunted tips. These lances were made of wood that would shatter on impact.

But even with these precautions, jousting was still a dangerous sport. During a tournament in 1559, the French king, Henry II, was struck by his opponent's lance. The lance shattered, just as it was supposed to. Unfortunately, it shattered inside the king's helmet. Wood splinters pierced his eye and brain, and King Henry died three weeks later. As a result, France declared jousting illegal.

Luckily, *Clocked!* takes place in Twigg, not France, and the story's good jousters survive their tournament (mostly) unharmed.